Jane Digby's Diary

For Mom and Dad

The heart has its reasons which reason knows not. - Blaise Pascal

1873

Damascus, Syria
June 24

When I look back on my life, I see some events as if they
happened five decades ago - others as if they had
happened the day before yesterday. I see Christmases
at Holkham Hall and classes at Tunbridge Wells dimly,
spurred only by my words before me. But I remember
distinctly, regardless of words, the face of George
Anson as he opens the door of my carriage, the dark
fingers of Lord Ellenborough as they interlace with
mine, and the broad smile of Felix Schwarzenberg
meeting our daughter for the first time. Time keeps
uneven pace, a mind's heart does not.

Inside an old woman hides the younger one.
Underneath her head of grey hair lie the memories of

one once red, brown, black, or gold. Recollection, though often piecemeal, may also conceal images indelible. And they may be made new again. Inside every woman, old or young, beats a rebel heart.

A Rebel Heart: Volume Two

1830

I am through with men.

I present my arguments here, my dear diary, my friend and sister confessor:

> Men lie. They tell you what you know is not true, but what you long to hear *until* you submit to their whispered nothings.

> They are vain. Though vanity is thought the fairer sex's province, men strut and preen more than the most beautiful of women.

Men boast. They know everything, even when they know little.

Men are greedy. They always want more - more money, more power - and, of course, more women.

They care less and are more careless than women. Self-absorption is their defining characteristic.

They are impatient. Nothing and no one is swift enough.

Men are stubborn and contrary, unwilling to compromise upon even the smallest matter.

Why *do* we love them, Marianne?

1831

Munich, Bavaria
March 20

Forgive me, Marianne. It has been more than six
months since my last confession - not that I have had
much opportunity to sin.

Lord and Lady Erskine were too kind upon my arrival,
allowing me to stay as their house guest in Munich until
I was able to find my feet. I was however introduced to
family and friends as Mrs. Eltham. We all thought it
best that I assume a name not associated with the
scandal I left behind me. Soon I longed for a place of
my own. The Erskines tried to dissuade me, but I was

determined to start afresh. With their help and knowledge of Munich, I rented a house just outside the city with a small garden and stable. It is from my new home that I write this entry.

I now immerse myself in the pleasures of making a comfortable life here - and the pleasures of living alone, with only Eugenie and a few servants as company. My independence from the demands of society allows me time for simple pleasures. I practice my German. I write terrible poetry. I read wonderful books. I play guitar and lute, lamenting my rusty skills at both. I sketch a late winter snowfall. When the weather permits I ride my new horse, a spirited gelding I call Mazeppa - after my favorite Byron poem - in Munich's largest park, the *Englischer Garten*.

I more often than not elude thoughts of London and Vienna.

March 30

A letter from Mama has arrived from London. I had written to her concerning my move just last week. The swiftness of her response makes me fear its contents. No matter how old I become or how many miles divide us, I fear my family's disapproval. And I know every letter from them holds it. They disapproved of my moving to Munich. They disapproved of my leaving Didi with Felix's sister, Matilde, in Vienna.

Now I learn that they disapprove of my living alone without the Erskines to act as chaperones. They worry for my reputation (or what little of it remains) and, of course, for my safety - neither of which is any concern to me. I live in a respectable neighborhood and live as quietly and as chastely as a nun. Mama tells me that Papa can hardly bear to hear my name spoken, though he tells her to ask me whether my very generous monthly allowance from my divorce settlement is sufficient for my needs. As if the weight of my guilt is not heavy enough, Marianne! Really, do all parents have that power over their wayward daughters?

Nevertheless, news from home is welcome. Mama tells me that my horse, Molly, is now part of Holkham's stables, where her gentle temperament makes her a favorite with my young cousins. My brother Edward continues his successful military career, while brother Kenhelm is soon to finish his university studies with plans to attend divinity school. Steely remains Mama's companion, though her sister, Jane, will soon marry a widowed clergyman from Dorset. Grandpapa has declined a peerage for the fifth time, this time from his old friend Earl Grey who is now Prime Minister since the Duke of Wellington's resignation. Grandpapa instead wishes, according to Mama, to remain "the greatest commoner in England." Meanwhile, Auntie Anne is busy planning her son's wedding. George Anson will marry Isabelle Forster this spring.

Tempus Fugit.

April 3

My twenty-fifth birthday passed pleasantly enough with a hired carriage ride with Eugenie through our new city. We toured the *Marienplatz* square with its medieval architecture and cobblestone streets, providing a sharp contrast with the new Greco-Roman architecture of the city's main thoroughfare, *Ludwigstrasse*. Bavaria's King Ludwig I is responsible for the construction of austere buildings such as *Odeon*, Munich's great concert hall and ballroom. The king is a creator and collector of all things neoclassical. Eugenie tells me it is rumored that he also collects women and has devoted a portrait gallery in his *Nymphenburg* palace to his numerous mistresses.

When we stopped at one of the many beer gardens along the Isar river for luncheon, we met a most amusing man who pretends (with little success) to be an Italian count. Before we left he slipped me a note written in Italian requesting a rendezvous tomorrow at The University of Munich, where he teaches his native language. I have no intention of meeting him, though Eugenie expressed an interest. I asked her what they could possibly talk about since he speaks only German and Italian, while she speaks only French and English. "The language of love, of course," she responded. And why not, my celibacy need not be shared!

April 10

I am enjoying vicariously Eugenie's not-so-secret love affair with *Sig* Alessandro Panzutti. She shares with me the intimate details of their lovemaking and that she uses a sea sponge dipped in vinegar as precaution against that near inevitable result of love. I confess her *Frankish* frankness makes me blush.

April 30

Felix and his sister have both written to me from Vienna.

Matilde tells me that at fifteen months, Didi is beginning to speak, but when she doesn't get what she wants soon enough, it leads to tantrums. Evidently my daughter has inherited my strong will and impatience.

Felix writes that his treatise about the 1830 revolution in Paris, which is now being called the *Trois Glorieuses*, or Three Glorious Days, has met with great success. Though I care nothing for politics and debate, I am happy that his political ambitions are thriving despite the scandal of our affair.

He says nothing about his daughter or our future. Though I am foolishly disappointed, I am not surprised.

May 10

With the urging of Eugenie and Alessandro, I am slowly entering society once again with Sunday afternoons and Wednesday evenings at *Tambosi's*, a popular coffeehouse near the *Holfgarten,* where Munich's intellectuals, musicians, writers, actors, and artists gather to discuss ideas and ideals. Such discussions to me are a welcome change from the gossip and intrigue of London and Paris. This lively renaissance Alessandro attributes to King Ludwig whose love of beauty influences the cultural milieu. In his quest to create the perfect city, the king is often seen strolling Munich, inspecting the progress of his many building projects with his architects and often stops to speak to anyone who catches his interest. He is, by all accounts, an uncommon man with a common touch.

May 22

I met Munich's uncommon man under the most unusual circumstances today, Marianne! Just as Eugenie and I sat down for coffee and cake *el fresco* at Tambosi's, a hush came over the establishment with only whispers of "*dos koenig*" breaking the silence, until a loud voice in English asked, "Madam, remove your veil, if you please." I quickly obliged and lifted my chin to look into the gentle gray eyes of King Ludwig.

"An English beauty, as I suspected?"

"Yes, Your Majesty," I responded.

"I urge the women of Munich to not wear veils. A face as lovely as yours should not be hidden."

"But Your Majesty, the veil protects this lovely face from the soot and dust of your streets."

The king laughed in response, showing large white teeth and replied, "Then an exception must be made, my dear." He then clicked his heels, bowed to me and nodded to Eugenie before taking his leave of us all.

Ten minutes later his manservant came back with a note in the king's hand, asking me to write down my name and address so that he might pay a call on me tomorrow at two!

May 23

I am nervous as the proverbial cat. As I await the king's arrival, I arrange and rearrange cut lilac blossoms. I call the chambermaid to dispatch a newly discovered cobweb hanging in a doorway. I check my appearance in the hallway mirror every five minutes. Only one o'clock! I force myself to sit and open my latest book,

The History of Mary Prince, but not even Mary's horrific tale of her enslavement can keep my attention. I turn then to you dear Marianne, in hopes of transferring my anxious thoughts to paper, only to have my fountain pen leak most annoyingly.

Now I shall meet the king with not only inky fingers, but with a black smudge across my left cheek!

May 24

My worry was for naught. The king was most charming during his call yesterday. He arrived promptly at two by coach without ceremony and immediately put me at ease with his self-deprecating humor. I apologized for my appearance, and he showed his own ink-stained hands - the result of "too much correspondence and too little soap," he claimed. He then demanded a tour of my modest home, stables, and gardens, or my "petite villa" as he most graciously deemed them.

Later, we sat for tea. Over pekoe and lemon-cheese tarts he asked me about my name, *Mrs.* Eltham. "Why is a married English woman living alone in Munich?" he asked. I confessed to my duplicity. In fact, I revealed the whole of my complicated and outrageous past. My marriage, divorce, and, of course, my affair with Prince Felix. The king was sympathetic to my story, seeing it as romantic and as moving as the fable of Tristan and Iseult. He vowed to help me regain Felix's love and demanded that I use my birth name - Jane Digby - once again.

Who am I to quarrel with a king?

June 12

It is so wonderful to have the companionship of a dear and kind friend - and that is what Lewis, as he insists I call him, has become to me. We meet three, sometimes four times a week and write to each other when we do not. I am his *Ianthe* - Jane in Greek. He is *Basily* - my king in the same. I find him a man of near-manic energy, an effect heightened by his booming voice. He tells me in confidence that a childhood bout with scarlet fever left him hard of hearing. I take special care to gain his attention before speaking, so that he has no cause to misunderstand me. We even exchange small gifts. Posies of violets to me. My latest sketches of Munich to him.

June 16

I must share Lewis's latest letter to me.

My dear Ianthe -

I have given much thought to your troubled past and your uncertain path to true love. I believe nothing truly worthwhile is gained without sacrifice, without pain. When we are young (and I speak as one twenty years older than you) we believe love will come to us as easily as spring follows winter. It sadly does not. For most of us love requires great struggle.

You became a victim of love. The world has exiled and judged you. I will not, because I understand. You seek a love as passionate as you. And you should accept nothing less.

Your Basily

I can scarcely believe how quickly and completely he has won my heart by dismissing the cruel conventions of the world to sympathize with me. It seems an incredible dream that I fear to trust.

June 20

Today I toured the building site of Munich's newest art museum, the *Pinakothek*, with the king. His enthusiasm was infectious, even amid the dust and noise. He reminds me of another king, King Coke. My grandfather insists upon supervising every detail of every project at Holkham. Like Lewis, he would even lay the stones, if the masons would allow him! And like my grandfather, Lewis commands the respect *and* the affection of his workers. I saw it in their eyes as he spoke with them, remembering their names, their trades. Such kingship cannot be taught.

Lewis also shared with me some of the royal art collection at the *Residenz Palace* that the Pinakothek will house upon its completion. He confessed to secreting some of his favorite works to his private apartments. One painting that most intrigued me was *Nude on a Sofa* by Francois Bucher. Its subject, according to Lewis, was the fourteen-year-old daughter of a prostitute, Marie-Louise O'Murphy, who later became King Louis XV of France's mistress. She made the unfortunate mistake of trying to replace the "official" mistress, the famed Madame de Pompadour, who convinced the king to remove Marie-Louis from court and marry her off to a soldier of good name but no fortune. The other painting, though without the intrigue, was even more fascinating, Albrecht Durer's *Self-Portrait*. Painted in 1500 at the age of 28, the artist's handsome face springs from the canvas with an intensity of gaze that haunts me - such is the power of great art.

My king also gave me a parting gift, a beautifully engraved prayer book, which he told me is identical to his own. When I expressed some surprise at his devoutness, he replied, "A passionate life and the life of the spirit are not mutually exclusive."

I did not have the heart to tell him that my own faith is unsure.

June 25

With the heat of summer upon us, Lewis and his court have moved to *Villa Ludwig Shohe*, his summer residence. He asked me to write to him, but advises that I take care with what I write, in deference to his Queen Therese. His concern and regard for her are strangely touching to me.

He also asked that I sit for a portrait by Joseph Stieler for his Gallery of Beauties in Palace Nymphenburg. He pronounces a Grecian theme a fitting one for my portrait, as he believes I represent its ideal - tall, gold, and strong.

Who am I to quarrel with a King?

July 6

I now spend my days first sitting for interminable hours in *Herr* Stieler's studio. I find it difficult to like him. Not a muscle may be moved without hearing an exasperated sigh from behind the easel. And not even a peek is allowed at the work in progress, though I must admit I do not like to share my own sketches before completion. I think to tell Mr. Stieler this, but I doubt whether he would appreciate the comparison. My poor scribblings compared to the works of the royal court painter. Indeed!

I then escape to the Holfgarten, riding as fast as Mazeppa and my clever new side-saddle, based upon the design of Jules Pellier, will allow. Its third pommel provides me a secure seat, enough that I can gallop and jump with ease. During one of my escapes I gained a new acquaintance and admirer, a baron from *Wurttemberg*, Karl Von Venningen.

Tall and red-haired, he flirts with me most outrageously, Marianne.

July 20

My portrait is finally finished. And although I feigned admiration to Herr Stieler, I do not like it. I stare from the canvas with such a placid simper that I consult the nearest mirror to reassure myself that I am not like. Thank God, the mirror tells me that the artist's skill and not my expression is at fault. How shall I ever find the words to describe my "appreciation" to Lewis!

July 30

I miss my dear friend. In his absence I spend my time with Karl. Though he is hardly the companion of heart and mind that Lewis is, I enjoy his admiration and the faithfulness of company. Every morning before the heat of the day pulls a damp blanket of humidity upon Munich, he meets me at the Englischer Garten where we ride until morning tea. He asks each morning to call on me later, but each morning I decline, saying that the king would disapprove. I suspect Karl believes the king and I are lovers, and I say and do nothing to dissuade him.

Why do I pretend, Marianne?

September 2

I am so sorry to have neglected you again, my dear. I have spent the last month restless and lonely. It is as if the whole world moves forward, while I am in some strange state of limbo with my past in retreat, but my future still unfolding. Even the baron and my lady's maid have deserted me! Karl to his estate in Weinheim, Eugenie to a much-earned holiday with Alessandro in the Bavarian Alps. However my solitude will end soon. Lewis writes that he will return to Munich within the week!

September 9

My reunion with the king was a curious one, Marianne.

It began pleasantly enough with his usual exuberance, as he told me of his latest acquisitions for his Pinakothek. He said little about his family or his retreat from Munich, but announced his admiration of my portrait which he has placed in his Gallery, declaring that Stieler captured my beauty most accurately. I artfully agreed that the painting was beautiful, but refrained from proclaiming my dislike of my rendering.

However, the mood quickly changed when he asked how I spent my last two months. I told him of my new acquaintance with Baron Von Venningen and our habit of riding each morning. His reaction was swift - and puzzling. He asked, "Do you forget your Prince so easily?" I replied, "Of course not," and promised to meet with Karl no longer.

I now wonder whether it is *my king* who worries that I forget *him*.

September 10

My mind keeps returning to that puzzling exchange.

September 11

Lewis will pay me a call tomorrow afternoon. I have a plan.

September 12

My plan went awry. Marianne. Let me set the pathetic scene for you:

I had decided that the king's anger with my meeting the Baron was due to his jealousy of Karl - and that I needed to make my availability to the King's affections clear.

I created what I thought was an irresistible scheme of seduction. I wore my most fetching afternoon dress and violet perfume. I dismissed the servants. I even inserted the *eponge* recommended by Eugenie in the certainty that all would go as I plotted. Unfortunately, that plot proved less than certain.

Lewis arrived promptly in his usual careless state of dress with his cravat hastily tied. I told him he could not sit to tea until I properly tied it for him. As I unknotted the cravat, I made sure to lightly brush his chin with my fingertips. After I pulled the ends straight, I looked deeply into his eyes and smiled. When I looped the ends over one another, I softly pressed my hand on his chest. In tying the bow, I inhaled and exhaled gently, allowing my breath to tickle his face. In applying the final adjustments, I murmured, "Now, you're handsome again."

His response to my not-so-subtle flirtation? A confused look that I failed to heed. After all, no man has ever rebuffed me. How could Jane Digby be resisted? I was soon to learn.

Embarrassing in retrospect were my subsequent actions. I played with a tendril of my hair when I laughed at his jokes. I stroked my face as I considered a response to a question. I boldly batted my eyes at his reply. Soon Lewis exclaimed, "What*ever* is wrong with you today, Jane?" Needless to say, my foolish plans were dashed.

I never *did* master the art of flirtation.

September 13

After Lewis made a hasty retreat yesterday, I could not stop thinking about my ridiculous display. Even now as the scene unfolds in my mind, my performance encores relentlessly, making me squirm and wince at my arrogant assumption concerning the king's affections.

I shall write to him immediately, asking him to forgive me.

September 16

Lewis's reply reassures me that our friendship remains. He only asks that I no longer "play act," pretending to be what I am not "when I am so much more."

How can I fail to love him, Marianne?

October 12

Oktoberfest. Today Munich celebrates the marriage of Ludwig I of Bavaria to Therese of Saxe-Hildburghausen.

Married in 1810, they celebrate their twenty-first year as husband and wife.

Meanwhile, Eugenie, Alessandro, and I enjoy the city in celebration. We stroll the beer and fish stands, sampling their wares. We watch as sixteen pairs of children in traditional lederhosen or dirndl represent the Bavarian provinces. They perform folk songs for the king and his lovely queen, who look to me like a perfect fairy tale as they sit with heads together and laugh as the children sing and dance. Later, we cheer on our favorite mount in the traditional two mile horse race and ride the carousel and swings. It is when we try our hands at the carnival booths with games of chance that I spot Baron Von Venningen, his ginger hair and broad shoulders towering above the crowd, watching us from a short distance away at the bowling lawn. Without thinking, I tell Eugenie not to wait for me, that I would find my own way home.

I spend the night with him. My long fast has finally ended.

Every day Karl asks me to marry him and every day I refuse him. It is a strange game we play. We meet at his lodgings in Munich, late afternoon into evening, though never again overnight. Sleeping together can be so much more intimate than the sexual act, and I feel I must keep my distance, not allow myself to fall again. Yet his body, pale and imposing, delights me. I trace its long line, following the gold hairs of arms, chest, and legs until he groans in impatience. I too am impatient.

November 2

All Souls' Day. I pray today for the Faithful Departed whom I do not forget - my friend Andriana and her Demetri, my dear cousin, Henry, and my darling son, Charlie. Still, I no longer pray for myself.

November 10

I am in the most utterly absurd position, Marianne. Lewis insists that I write Felix to ask him to meet me at *Jagdschloss*, one of many hunting lodges in Wurttemberg owned by the king. This plan for our intimate *rendezvous* was only the latest scheme concocted by the king to reignite the flame of Felix's love for me. How can I tell Lewis my hope for a conciliation with the prince is faint. But how can I possibly refuse the king? And how can I explain my absence to the baron, who becomes more possessive of me with each passing day?

Just another scrape in the life of Jane Digby.

November 12

As Lewis suggested, I have written Felix about my plan to vacation at the Jagdschloss near Calw later this month and have asked whether he might join me there to discuss a reconciliation. To my shame, I lied to Karl, telling him that I would be visiting my daughter, Didi, in Vienna for a fortnight.

November 26

I pack for Jagdschloss. I leave on the morrow.

The Road to Jagdschloss
November 27

I write this entry as I travel alone - Eugenie remains in Munich with her Alessandro - through the Black Forest by hired coach. With its high slopes, streams, and deep woods, I can see why this land is subject to dark fables and superstitions. It is as if I ride through a Grimm's fairy tale - any moment Rumpelstiltskin, The Pied Piper, or Little Snow White and her Dwarves might appear before me. I remember as a young girl being told the tale, *The Little Glass Slipper*, in which Cinderella finds her Prince.

I too once found my prince, but now fear he is forever lost to me.

Calw, Wurttemberg
November 28

I arrived earlier today. Jagdschloss is a most handsome lodge with a decidedly masculine appearance - rich wood, brown leather furnishings, and a massive stone fireplace completed with a brown bear rug lying before it. Fortunately, no animal trophies mar its walls. Is there anything more dreadful than seeing lifeless creatures serve as decoration? Instead, informal portraits of the king's ancestors look down at me with his same small smile.

November 29

As I thought, Felix will not join me. He sent his regrets by messenger, a young boy from nearby Calw. I asked him to wait while I composed a short message to Lewis, telling him that the prince would not be joining me, though I wished to remain at Jagdschloss for the next week to consider my future.

December 1

It has been so long since I have been truly alone - and I find I enjoy it. I sit here by the window with a hot cup of tea with only you and my guitar for company, a light snow falls adding to my pleasant solitude. I drift into a light sleep until I am awakened by a muted clatter of carriage wheel. I throw open the window for a better look at my visitor.

It is the king.

December 4

We have spent our days and our nights together, Marianne, and I have never experienced such a union of mind, body and spirit. We walk through new fallen snow, savoring the chill bite of the air and the woolen silence that envelops the forest. With no servants to wait upon us we prepare simple meals: rye bread and mustard with *leberswurst* and *butterkase*. We sleep together with limbs entwined under eiderdown to ward off the cold and damp of late autumn, until Lewis feeds the fire on the hearth. My king reads me tales from Hebel's *The Treasure Chest* in his strong tenor; I play guitar and sing English ballads. With no one to see or hear us, we make love upon the bear rug until we are spent and sated - for a time.

Our worlds seem so far away now.

December 7

Today I asked Lewis why he came to me. He replied that at first he thought that he did not wish for me to be alone, knowing that he bore much of the responsibility for my being here with his insistence that I plan a lover's tryst with Felix. But with each mile he traveled he slowly realized that it was not the tryst that he misjudged, but rather the lover.

How can I not love him, Marianne?

December 12

Today we depart Jagdschloss. Before we leave by separate coaches, Lewis tells me he will write me each day, but again urges me to take care in my replies. I ask when we will meet again. He tells me that during the holiday celebrations his duties as king will make that difficult, but promises he will try.

I fear being mistress to a king requires patience, a virtue, as you well know, with which I have little acquaintance.

Munich, Bavaria
December 16

Lewis has written me a most charming letter, though he never mentions our time at his hunting lodge or anything of an intimate nature. I reply in an equally guarded manner, though I mention (merely in passing, of course) seeing Baron Von Venningen at Tambosi's.

December 18

My little white lie achieved its desired effect. Lewis paid a call this afternoon.We spent the afternoon in each other's arms, unguarded and unclothed.

December 24

I spend my first Christmas Eve alone, surrounded by cards and letters from family and friends in London. Their writing helps ease my loneliness but their words, though they can sustain my heart and mind, cannot give me the lines of a face, the sound of a voice, or the touch of a hand. I must recall each line, sound, and touch, though time and distance obscures each one.

December 25

What I feared might have been a lonely holiday was eased by three unexpected events. The first was preceded by a soft knock at the door. With Cook and her staff busy preparing Christmas goose, I answered it to find a young boy with a wicker basket topped by a red and green bow. Inside was a King Charles Spaniel, a gift from Lewis. I gave the boy a gulden to send him on his way then eagerly read the note tied round the dog's neck: "From one king I give another to my dearest Ianthe. From your Basily."

Next was the early return of Eugenie and Alessandro from a visit to his family's home. My dear friends did not wish for me to spend Christmas day alone. And finally, the third unexpected event was introduced by a second knock at my door. I opened it to find Baron Von Venningen. Karl said that he would only stay a moment, but wanted to wish me a *Frohe Weihnachten*. I convinced him to stay for dinner, and we all celebrated the season with goose, pudding, and cider, singing carols in an eccentric but enthusiastic mix of English, German, French, and Italian.

December 26

I wake to the sound of a soft snore and a warm body next to mine. No, my dear, my companion is not Karl, who I sent away last night with my consent to call next week, but instead my gift from Lewis whom I have named Tuilly. A young male with a spaniel's distinctive white and red markings, he also possesses the breed's sweet disposition, but unfortunately, as I have just learned, is not housebroken.

1832

Munich, Bavaria

January 1

I have spent my Christmastide training Tuilly. I, or a reluctant chambermaid, brave cold weather to take him outside five times a day. I even startle him midstream with a clap and hustle him outside to complete the job. All the while I wait for word from Lewis.

Xj F zlkcrpfkd lkb hfqj clo xklqebo, Jxofxkkb?

January 2

Unlike the king, the baron has not forgotten me. Karl visited earlier today, arriving with an enormous bouquet of fragrant lilies from his own greenhouse in Weinheim. As I arranged them in my largest vase, he circled my waist with his arms, planting soft kisses on the nape of my neck. He asked whether we might retire to my bedchamber. I replied, "Yes, if you promise not to ask me to marry you." To which *he* replied, "For today, at least."

January 10

The king and I parted with harsh words after he paid me a call today. To my surprise, he learned that I had been entertaining the baron. I asked him how he came upon such knowledge and whether he was having me watched. He answered that there was no need, since we were conducting our affair with no discretion.

He made it abundantly clear that he would share me with no man.

January 12

After much thought I wrote to Lewis telling him that I would no longer see the baron. I wrote: "I am ready to give my word not to yield any more, for to cut with *you*, I cannot, will not."

Now I must tell Karl.

January 13

My meeting with the baron was an unmitigated disaster. I told him of the king's wishes concerning me, and that I would like Karl's word that he would promise to pursue me no longer. It was in vain. Neither entreaties nor threats could prevail upon him. He answered that it was impossible for him to give his word of honour, and that he loved me, would always love me, and would never, even for a king, renounce his claim upon me.

Really, how could I resist such a passionate declaration?

January 14

Today, I shall give our absurd love triangle a thorough examination, Marianne. I shall think the problem through with numerical reasoning.

The case for Baron Von Venningen:

1. He loves me and wishes to marry me.
2. He is titled and wealthy with numerous estates which he administers with care.
3. Though a woman of discrimination really should not consider a man's looks to be paramount, I must admit the baron is a perfect physical specimen: tall, fair, and handsome.
4. He loves horses and the outdoors, as I do.
5. He is attentive. In fact, he allows me to lead our conversations, so much so that I dominate them. I have asked him whether my chattering away bothers him, but he replied that he likes talkative women. A convenient state of affairs, I must say.
6. His attentiveness extends to the bedroom. Need I say more?
7. I do not love him.

The case for King Ludwig:

1. He is a dear friend and confidant but is another woman's husband.
2. Though wealthy, the King of Bavaria is a dreadful spendthrift.
3. Despite his age, he is an attractive man, possessing a wonderful sense of humor.
4. We both are intellectually curious: we share a love of art, music, poetry and books.

5. He runs hot; he runs cold. Some days he cannot bear to part with me, others he is distant and cool.
6. I love him, Marianne.

January 16

I have broken with Karl, as my king bids me.

February 2

Midwinter. I bide my time as the king bids me, though I find his absences too long and my days even longer.

March 1

As spring approaches, Munich awakes from a long winter. With the melting snow and longer days, Lewis is even more preoccupied with his city and his ceaseless building projects.

He still has little time for me.

March 10

I have just received a most disturbing letter from an
Italian Marchesa, Marianna Florenzi, who claims to be
the king's mistress. She also claims to know of my
scandalous past and demands that I no longer see
Lewis, or she will tell him of my "lascivious reputation."
Her attempt at blackmail is of course futile, since I have
already revealed all to him. Now, I must ask Lewis the
nature of his relationship with her!

March 12

I wrote to the king concerning the Marchesa, and he, in
reply, orders me not to concern myself with her. He
fails to explain their relationship in any way. I must
assume that they are indeed lovers. Evidently,
exclusiveness is demanded of me, but not of him,
Marianne.

March 20

As I lay in Karl's arms after our lovemaking, he asks me
again to marry him. I again say no. "If he were not a

king, I would challenge him to a duel," he replies. I order him not to speak of the king, saying that I will leave and not return. He agrees not to speak of him - if I stay the night.

I do.

April 1

From whence came the custom of making the first of April the day for fools?

Is it, as I have been told, from the town of Gotham in Nottinghamshire? According to legend, the town, in an effort to prevent unpopular King John from visiting, pretended to drown fish and pen birds in roofless cages. They did so to gain a reputation as a place too foolish to warrant the king's notice.

Or is it, as I suspect, a day to declare spring after dark winter, to become drunk with bright days, to find the arms of one lover in the warmth of the afternoon and seek the arms of another to warm the cool nights.

I am a fool of April.

April 3

My twenty-fifth birthday. I received a bouquet of fragrant violets from Lewis and yellow roses from Karl, as well as letters from home. Among the correspondence was an unexpected letter from Princess Esterhazy, my old friend from London. She wrote of Felix and suggests that a reconciliation may be possible if I swear that I never took Monsieur Lambeau, who you may remember acted as my escort during my pregnancy with Didi, as my lover. *Really?* I am to swear *again* that a man who I can barely even recall was never my lover! If I were the suspicious type, I might think the princess is trying to create more melodrama for London society's entertainment. Or perhaps, to be more charitable, she might feel some guilt for her own role in driving Felix and me apart. Either way I no longer seek Felix's love.

Besides, how could I possibly have the stamina for *three* lovers?

April 15

Another letter has arrived from the king. Lewis has learned of "the continued presence" of the baron in my life, and again demands that I break with him.

I write back immediately to Lewis defending Karl and our relationship once more. I remind him that he told me to never expect more than he could give in our relationship. He *therefore* must forgive me for seeking more from another.

April 23

It has been over a week, and the king has not answered my letter. I fear I have forever lost my dear friend to hasty words.

I shall write again.

April 24

I just posted my letter to Lewis, asking him to forgive my harsh words. I asked that we might remain friends, though we may never again be more.

April 28

Not a word from Lewis.

May 7

Though I have not told Karl of my break with the king, he is nevertheless enjoying my undivided attention. I ride with him all fair mornings and spend nearly every evening together, whether fair or foul. He has taken to calling me "his Jeanne." I really am very fond of him, Marianne.

I ask myself, why can't I love him? Is because I crave the melodrama of the love triangle in which I find myself. If that is indeed the case then I should be happy with the state of affairs - but I am not.

I try to reason, but my heart resists my attempt.

May 10

After more than two weeks Lewis has finally written to me. He tells me that we will always remain friends, though he believes that it may be best for all involved that we remain *only* friends.

May 20

Though I thought I was taking adequate precautions, I am late. I have counted the days to make sure.

Nduo lv vxuhob wkh idwkhu.

May 30

I will tour Italy, while I am still free to do so. Eugenie and I have spent the last few days packing for our journey. I swear I am becoming more and more like La Madre. I so hate the thought of leaving the comforts of home that I attempt to carry them all with me. Linens,

Limoge, and crystal. My small library. Sketch books and watercolors. My guitar and lute. Wardrobes for both cool and hot weather, since we travel through the Alps to Genoa to Naples, perhaps as far as Palermo, Sicily. And Tuilly, of course. Will one coach be enough for it all?

Eugenie complains, swearing softly in a colorful mix of Italian and French. She will miss her Alessandro, though he will meet us in Genoa during his university leave.

I have told only Eugenie of my interesting condition.

The Road to Genoa
June 5

It has been nearly eight years since I have seen the Alps. Their cold beauty still delights. I have decided to stop for a few days at a small inn near Lausanne to capture that beauty with both charcoal and watercolor. Perhaps I'll send a sketch or two to Mama and Papa to remind them of our trip so many years ago. Just the thought of them brings me tears. Why ever am I so weepy of late?

I suppose we both know the answer to that question, Marianne.

Genoa, Italy

June 10

Is there any feeling more exhilarating than arriving at a destination unknown? I heard Papa speak of Genoa as a great port city. He had visited it often during his duties as Rear-admiral, but I never saw this pink and gold city on the Mediterranean, or its surrounding regions, for myself.

We have rented an *appartamenti* in Liguria on the Italian coastline for the summer months, but for now Eugenie and I will spend the week touring the city.

June 16

As planned, we toured Genoa all this week and walked *Strade* and *Strada* to see *Plazarri* and *Plazarro* through medieval gates, mazes of grand squares, and narrow alleys filled with street vendors hawking their wares. An untidy jumble of pastel and portico homes contrasted with the grace of *Boccadasse* harbor. There colorful boats were sailed by loose-limbed sailors who expertly navigated the wharves. It is an ancient city alive with present-day commerce and trade.

Today we stopped at a street food shop to eat green *pesto* and savory *focaccia* followed by a sweet *gelato* before we completed our tour to see the Holy Chalice of Genoa at the cathedral of Saint Lorenzo. Thought by the Genoese to be the Holy Grail used by Christ during the Last Supper, the green glass chalice shines as bright as an emerald - and with an unlikely elegance. Perhaps it is my Anglican cynicism, but I wonder how Christ, a poor carpenter, came to use such an object?

I suppose one should not ask such questions, Marianne.

Portofino, Liguria
June 19

It is early twilight. I sit here on our terrace sipping *espresso* as I look out over the Mediterranean Sea with Tuilly napping at my feet. All the *riviera*, as the sea's coastline is called by locals, is astonishingly beautiful. But most beautiful of all is the fishing village of *Portofino*. Soft pastel buildings surround a small harbor of azure blue where small sailing boats bob gently. The sharp consonants and cadence of Italian and the scent of tangy saltwater combine with the chatter of circling terns who hover above the boats in search of scraps thrown by the fishermen. The dark soon settles. Pink sky turns gray. Consonance and chatter end. I drain my cup.

June 30

The days pass here with a sameness that does not bother me. Even Eugenie, who at first questioned why we bury ourselves here, has surrendered to the calm. We spend our idylls scouring the beach at nearby *Paraggi* to look for seashells. Barefoot we tuck the hems of our skirts in our waistbands like local fishwives to avoid the wet of the surf. Tuilly chases seagulls.

After filling my basket with my treasures, I sit on the sand and watch the surf, spotting a family of dolphins jumping from the water - one young dolphin no bigger than a dinner plate. I hear Eugenie in the distance shout "Jane" as she waves me to her. I cross the sand to see what she has discovered: a sea turtle laying eggs in the sand. By the day's afterglow we watch as mother turtle spends nearly an hour there, using her flippers to cover her nest with sand.

Too soon is the time for us to leave. The full moon rises as we walk the mile long path to the villa, sunburned despite our bonnets.

July 4

I spent this stormy day in correspondence. Thunder and lightning provided a backdrop to my thoughts. First, I wrote my family in England. Second, I wrote

Felix in Paris. Third, Matilde and Didi in Vienna. Fourth, the king. Fifth, the baron.

To each I disguised my reasons, claiming boredom and capriciousness to explain my flight to Italy. They will learn the truth soon enough.

July 10

Alessandro has arrived from Munich much to Eugenie's delight. They will spend a week here, then tour Venice with my blessing. I plan to spend my days capturing Italian light with my watercolors and walking Tuilly on the beach, and my evenings reading George Sand's novel, *Lelia*. She (George Sand is the nom de plume of Amantine Lucile Dupin) has scandalized Paris with her habit of dressing as a man and with her radical ideas concerning the rights of women. I do hope the novel is as fascinating as the author.

July 19

Karl has followed me to Liguria. He arrived yesterday, clearly unsure as to how I might regard his surprise visit. But as usual his devotion won me over. Like so many large men, he is gentle and kind. Perhaps his stature allows him a confidence that eludes smaller men. It is his most attractive quality.

We typically spend our days walking the beach, but one day he convinced a local fisherman to rent his sailboat - for an exorbitant fee - so that we might yacht upon the Mediterranean. His skill as a sailor surprised me. He told me that he often sailed on Lake Chiemsee during summers as a boy. As Karl faced the wind while holding sail, I could easily imagine him as one of his ancestors, a Viking warrior set upon a journey to explore new worlds. I told him so, knowing the thought would please him.

I have not told him that I carry his child.

July 24

The days pass quickly here. I keep losing them. What happened to Sunday, to Tuesday or Thursday? What is the date? Is July really almost over? Karl tells me to hush. He does not want to be reminded that he must leave early next month to attend his estates. I have until then.

July 31

I could wait no longer.

This morning, as we lie beneath the tangle of sheets thrown off from the heat of our lovemaking, I tell him that I am pregnant with his child, that I am certain. He is delighted and, without hesitation, begins plans for the future. He wants us to leave Italy immediately for Weinheim to meet his family and to marry before the child makes its presence known to all.

He believes the child will bind me to him. Of that I am not certain.

August 5

I stall. I have told Karl that I need time to think, that I wish to stay in Liguria until the end of my lease with Eugenie who just yesterday returned with Alessandro. We quarrel and although he tries repeatedly, he cannot convince me to return with him.

August 7

Both Karl and Alessandro left reluctantly this morning for their obligations in Germany. The villa is quiet without their presence. Gone is Karl's loud tread as he leaps two steps at time up the staircase to our suite. Gone is the sound of Alessandro's voice as he sings the role of Figaro in *The Barber of Seville*. Though I enjoy the quiet, Eugenie complains of it. She asks that we follow the men to Germany or, at the very least, travel from here to Sicily sooner than we planned.

After some thought I agree to move on to Sicily. We must travel while I still can.

Naples, Italy

August 20

Eugenie and I have arrived at Naples by coach. Two women alone and bound for adventure. From here we travel by boat to Palermo, Sicily, but not until we tour the ruins of nearby Pompeii day after next.

August 22

Early yesterday, before the worst of Italian summer heat, we hired a coach to take us the short distance to Pompeii. We walked the abandoned streets of a city silenced over 1,800 years ago. It is as if we strolled a cemetery where past lives are buried under the ash of a volcano. I wondered, can the dead in unmarked graves rest in peace?

The sound of male voices ended my morbid thoughts. We came across some students from Oxford here for their Grand Tour. They told us that they would hike

Mount Vesuvius tomorrow; their young faces shone, eager at the prospect of a challenge.

I do so wish I could join them. Alas, my corset and my delicate condition prevent me.

Palermo, Sicily

August 30

We have finally settled in at our destination, a home rented from an Italian aristocrat who spends the year in the Americas. As I recover from the sea voyage, I finally finish reading, *Lelia*. What a complicated heroine, perhaps as complex as the authoress herself. In the novel Leia, though once a woman with many lovers, becomes cynical about romance, claiming it a trap laid by men to ensnare women to their desires. This change of heart causes her to spurn the attention of a young poet who, as a result, comes to a tragic end.

Is the author alerting her reader to the dangers of love, or is she warning them not to become cynical about love? I, for one, hope never to lose faith in love's power. As Sand herself says, "There is only one happiness in life, to love and be loved."

September 2

I again write to family and friends, Lewis and Karl included, to inform them of my change in plans and that Eugenie and I expect to spend the fall and winter in Palermo to benefit from the mild winters here. I have told no one but Eugenie and Karl of my pregnancy.

September 10

We spend our days as all pilgrims in Palermo do, with *Monte Pellegrino* looming over our every step. Johann Wolfgang von Goethe has called it "the most beautiful promontory in the world" in his *Italian Journey* which I carry with me as a tourist might a tour book. Eugenie finds my preoccupation with "a dead German writer" perplexing. My attempts to explain to her that Goethe's goal as a traveler - to discover one's self in what one sees - should be our goal too here in Palermo. She responds disdainfully, saying that she has no interest in discovering herself and even if she were, she would hardly try to find herself in an object!

Who am I to argue with French logic?

September 20

Marianne, may I take this moment to speak about Italian, particularly Sicilian, men? These men are, based upon my observations these past weeks, great lovers of life and of feminine beauty. Every gesture, word, and glance is imbued with *joie de vivre* - except in Italian. Take, for example, our encounter with a group of admirers while strolling the grounds of *Villa Palagonia* - a Baroque villa famous for its grotesque statues of monster and human composites, over six hundred in total. Amid leering stares of gnomes, cherubs, aristocrats, nobles, and gargoyles, our admirers offered a handsome contrast to the madness of the villa's cast of characters. *Ciao, le mie bellezzaro*, said one young man whose dark eyes twinkled with good humor. Another added, *Dacci un bacio*, as he ogled us.

Over five months along, I found their attentions a balm to my spirit.

September 25

One of our Italian admirers from the Villa Palagonia named Federico proves most persistent, though both Eugenie and I have sworn to one another not to encourage his efforts. He has repeatedly tried to enter the house disguised as a woodcutter, a travelling musician, even a friar. Each time he is discovered and ejected despite his protestations of love - though he will not say to whom he has lost his heart. No doubt he hopes that either Eugenie or I (or perhaps both?) will succumb to his ardent efforts!

Karl has written that he will arrive in Palermo by the end of the week. Lewis too writes, at long last, asking when I shall return to Munich.

September 30

Karl arrived from Munich earlier this morning. However Frederico timed his weekly routine to this arrival, resulting in a most unfortunate encounter. Let me set the scene for you:

Just as Karl kisses me hello and whispers his admiration of my new voluptuousness, we both hear a loud growl from Tuilly. Eugenie joins us to investigate the source of the dog's annoyance, and we find that he has cornered Frederico, dressed as a chimney sweep, in the sitting room. Upon seeing us, Frederico bolts to the door in an attempt to flee my imposing lover (and a snarling spaniel) but is easily captured by Karl. Eugenie and I then must explain the situation before blows are struck. Our explanations do little to defuse the situation, in fact Karl becomes even more agitated. But as he prepares to strike a blow, the agile Frederico manages to escape, running past us and through the open front door with Karl and Tuilly in pursuit. Eugenie shouts, "Run, Frederico," and we both laugh until we are in tears.

Tuilly returns in a matter of minutes, with Karl soon after, empty-handed and breathless. Eugenie and I manage - just barely - to contain our laughter.

October 3

The incident with Frederico forgotten, Karl asks that we marry before the birth of our child. I tell him that we should wait, so that we might marry in Germany without embarrassment. Pleased that I have finally agreed to marry him, he sees the wisdom in our waiting, though he insists that he stay with me until after the birth. How can I not appreciate his faithfulness to me?

I have written to Lewis to tell him of my adventures in Italy and that I plan to spend the winter. I make no mention of my pregnancy, or of Karl and his presence here.

November 30

I apologize once again for my neglect of you, Marianne, though I have so little to say of any interest. I can only complain - that I grow too stout, that my ankles swell to the size of my knees, that my back aches continually. I see Eugenie and Karl bit their tongues at my grousing, but I cannot seem to stop.

I cannot *wait* for this dreadful business to be over.

December 10

Karl has engaged the services of a midwife for the birth, an old Italian woman who speaks serviceable English and who claims to have delivered over one hundred children, having never lost a mother or child. Her experience reassures me much but her manner more so. She examines me thoroughly, declaring both mother and child healthy and adds that the child should arrive by the end of next month. I ask her, half jokingly, whether it be a boy or a girl. She answers, "I am a midwife, not a seer, *cara signora*."

December 25

Karl and I spend a quiet Christmas here in Palermo. Eugenie again travels with her Alessandro to his family home for the holiday season. Before she departs she reveals to me that they hope to marry by the end of next year, when they have saved enough money to buy a home in the Munich countryside. The thought of losing her troubles me, but I say nothing to cool her delight.

The warmth of the Italian sun makes for a pleasant, though peculiar, holiday season. We can walk - in my case, waddle - about without hats, gloves, or overcoats. In fact the air seems more April than December during the entire *Novena*, the nine days celebrated by all Italians to commemorate the journey of the Magi to the manger of the Christ child.

Karl surprises me with a beautiful collection of Charles Lamb essays and Victor Hugo's *Hunchback of Notre Dame* which has, I hear, met with great success in Paris. I give him a handsome shaving kit which I hope will encourage him to shave his chin beard. Do men *really* consider such beards attractive?

1833

Epiphany eve. *La Befana*, the wise-woman, brings gifts to children on this night, according to Italian tradition. Tonight I sit reading the last chapter of Victor Hugo's novel aloud, while a *beardless* Karl builds a fire, the first one we have needed all winter. Its crackle and snap accompanies the tragic love story of the beautiful Esmeralda and Quasimodo. Years ago, Victor told me that he would one day write a great novel about his lady of Paris, Notre-Dame, and he has.

I am glad his dream came true.

February 20

I have given Karl a son named Herberto. His birth was not an easy one, despite the skill of Sophia who has taken the child to be nursed and fostered by one of her granddaughters. Though he was born over three weeks ago, I have only just now had the strength to sit up and put pen to paper. I was struck by a fever so fierce both Karl and Eugenie feared for my life. Only Sophia's efforts saved me, they claim. She pressed damp cloths upon my body until the fever broke. She then fed me cold tomato soup, spoonful by spoonful, as I laid in bed, weak as a kitten.

Now, my body has recovered, though a strange despondency seeps into my every thought. I cry without provocation. I cannot sleep. Sophia insists that I drink sage and peppermint tea, a ghastly concoction that she insists will ease my worry.

March 10

With the coming of spring, the worst of my nagging melancholy has left me and has been replaced with some small measure of optimism for the future. Karl, who has rarely left my side, asks that we return to Germany next month to his family's estate in Weinheim, so that I might meet his family.

How can I deny him, Marianne? His concern and love for me has created a debt that I must repay.

March 14

All the necessary letters have been written and our itinerary planned.

I have asked Karl whether we might stop in Venice for my birthday before travelling on to Weinheim and he, always hoping to please me, agreed. We will travel alone. Eugenie has already returned to my home in Munich, eager to be united with Alessandro. Herberto is too young for such a journey, and frankly his presence would very much complicate matters. He will be left to the expert care of dear Sophia until our return.

Venice, Italy

April 3

My twenty-sixth birthday - in Venice. I am convinced
there is no more romantic city on earth. Karl and I
spent the day as lovers do. We climbed St. Mark's
Campanile and toured the *Basilica*. We walked the
Rialto Bridge and shopped its market. We floated the
Grand Canal, where swarthy *gondoliers* rowed their
traditional flatboats with sweeping prows. I asked our
gondolier whether he might sing for us, as the stories
have it. "Madame," he responded with an arch look,
"there are lovers and there are singers. I am a lover."

Later, after dinner at our hotel, we walked along
Cannaregio Canal until Karl suggested we sit on a bench
that overlooked the water. The evening afterglow and
rising moon shone upon us. He turned to me, covered
one of my hands with one of his own, and clearing his
throat said:

"Jane, you know that I am a man of action not words. For this reason, I borrow words that you may recognize . . .

'You pierce my soul. I am half agony, half hope. I offer myself to you again. I have loved none but you. For you alone, I think and plan. You may not believe that there is true attachment and constancy in men. However, I ask that you believe them most fervent, most undeviating in me.'

"Will you marry me?"

As Frederick Wentworth convinces Anne Elliot in Jane Austen's *Persuasion*, so does Karl Von Venningen convince Jane Elizabeth Digby.

April 10

Before we leave Italy, Karl and I set ourselves to the difficult task of writing letters to our families, revealing our plans for marriage and the birth of our child.

I also write to the king revealing the same.

April 20

As we complete our preparations for our departure to Weinheim, letters from home find us. First, my mother writes, confessing her surprise at my news, remarking that "most daughters seek marriage before children" but knowing my "willful nature" she should be content in the knowledge that a marriage was "thought necessary at all." She also hopes that I "count my blessings" in finding a man such as the baron who offers me not only marriage, but "an opportunity to return to respectable society."

La Madre can always be counted upon for her unsolicited advice.

Lewis also expresses surprise at the content of my letter, but declares the situation "the best for all involved." He asks that I write again before we exchange vows, so that we might send "his Ianthe an appropriate wedding gift." He signs his note, "Your Basily."

The King can always be counted upon for his generosity, and his ambivalence.

Karl's mother also writes, but he refuses to discuss her letter in any detail, saying only that his family is "displeased" with our news, but assures me that since his father's death, he is the head of the family and will not allow their displeasure to interfere with our plans.

An auspicious beginning for the happy couple, Marianne!

Weinheim, Wurttemberg
May 1

May Day in Weinheim. Karl and I arrived late last night under the cover of darkness with only a few sleepy servants to attend us. This morning however I awoke to Teutonic efficiency - our coffee served promptly at nine with a breakfast of *Brot* and *Brotchen* decorated with butter, jam, and honey. Precisely at eleven our mounts were readied for my tour of his family home and estate.

Karl's love of growing things was evident in his arboretum where numerous trees and shrubs, both common and uncommon, dominate the landscape - and in his greenhouses where he and his gardeners practice plant breeding to produce what he called *hybrids*, or new varieties of flowers.

Later we rode to a hilltop which overlooked the town and the Rhine valley where we saw gingerbread houses with steeply pitched roofs of red and acres of vineyards in flower. I challenged him to a race back to the *schloss*, our country home. I am victorious, though I strongly suspect Karl allowed me the win.

Curiously, his kind duplicity irritates me.

May 5

I met Karl's mother and sister yesterday when we paid a call to their home, a family estate, in Gromach.

Evidently my reputation precedes me. Their cool disdain was barely hidden by their forced smiles and hooded eyes. Karl gamely tried to melt their icy manner by speaking of our travels in Italy, while I chattered on about my family in England, especially my grandfather. I suppose I thought to impress them with his wealth and reputation, but only succeeded in looking a fool. After this mercifully short visit, Karl apologized for their behavior and begged me to give them more time to get better acquainted. He predicts that they will grow to love me.

I sincerely doubt that, though I say nothing.

May 12

Mama writes again to ask that we might meet in Paris next month. I am eager for a change of pace, and for the chance to see her and Steely once again. Has it really been nearly two years since I last saw them? And the timing could not be more perfect, since Karl is managing his other estates in June and will have little time for me. I also thought I might pay a call to Matilde and my daughter, Didi, in Vienna. I shall write to both Mama and Matilde, *sofort*.

Paris, France
June 1

Since my arrival in Paris, I have been haunted by
memories of my past here. A sweet son's death. An ugly
divorce. A revolution erupted and ended. A love affair
evanesced. Bygone events dog my every step. I resist
the temptation to contact Felix who continues his
diplomatic work here.

My dark mood has even colored my reunion with my
mother and Steely. Mama has grown plumper, Steely
thinner. Both have aged, and I fear I am the cause of
more than one or two of their grey hairs. We talk of
family. Grandfather has retired from Parliament, but
remains hale as ever. Father has been promoted to
Vice-admiral, a promotion that requires him to spend
even more time away from Forston. Brother Edward
continues his military career in the Yeoman Cavalry.
Dear Kenhelm hopes to become Vicar at Tittleshall. And
Steely's sister, Jane, is soon expecting her first child.
Mama asks after Karl - asks when she and Papa will
meet him, when we will marry, and when they will see

Herberto. I answer her questions as obliquely as I can. I think before I speak, a rarity for me.

After we part, I try not to feel relief.

Vienna, Austria

June 10

My mood has followed me from Paris to Vienna.

I had spent the remainder of my time with Mama and
Steely in constant motion. With every meeting I
suggested excursions. We toured the *Louvre*, strolled
the shops on the *Champ Elysees*. I even convinced them
to ride the *Champ de Mars* carousel. We laughed like
schoolgirls with each merry go round. Not once, to my
relief, did we speak of the past or the future.

Tomorrow I see my daughter again.

June 11

I must write while I remember each detail, Marianne.

Matilde had not changed. The same crooked smile and
lovely eyes, so similar to her brother's. Didi however
had. The baby I left was now a toddler, a chubby

towhead with a dimpled chin. I could see neither me nor Felix in her unformed features, but I could see her fear of me, as she hid behind her namesake's skirts. I know it natural for a young child to shy from strangers, but I must admit my disappointment..

She spoke of Felix's success as a diplomat. I spoke of Karl and our engagement, and of our son. We passed the afternoon cordially enough - until it was time for me to leave. I asked when I might see Didi again and she replied,

"Perhaps it is best that you do not, my dear. It would only confuse Didi as she grows older, and she would certainly learn of the scandal surrounding her birth - and after all you have a new family."

Shocked, I said nothing in response.

Munich, Bavaria

June 14

I have returned to Munich, greeted by Eugenie and a persistent Tuilly who refuses to leave me out of his sight. It is good to be home, though my mind keeps returning to Vienna. I try to escape my thoughts by riding Mazeppa, who has grown quite fat in my absence, in the Englischer Garten.

There is a cruel logic to Mathilde's final words. Yes, Didi would be better off not knowing the circumstances of her birth. Yes, if all goes as planned, I shall be busy with my "new family." Even my heart tells me Didi would be happier in Vienna, but my heart also wishes it to be otherwise.

A woman's heart can be a duplicitous thing.

June 20

Karl and I have reunited. He presented me with a Renaissance ancestor's gimmel engagement ring, a gold ring encrusted with rubies, emeralds, and sapphires consisting of two hoops that fit together to form one ring. He will wear one half. I, the other. I asked how the family could part with it. He said that his mother was reluctant, until he told her that he would give his Gromach estate to her and his sister, who is unlikely to marry, in exchange. Such a lovely gesture. Such a clever man.

June 30

I find myself still stalling. I cannot, will not, name a date for our wedding, despite Karl's insistence that I do so. My latest effort at procrastination involved using Papa as an excuse. I told Karl that I wished for my father to attend the ceremony, as it would go far in healing the rift between us. However Papa would not be able to attend the ceremony until November, when he returns from his duties at sea. Karl reluctantly agreed, but demanded no more postponements. He is eager to begin married life - and to begin *his* duties as husband and father. Our son, Herberto, will remain in Italy until the nuptials.

July 11

Lewis writes to tell me he misses his Ianthe and asks when we might meet. I know I should refuse, but I cannot - will not - Marianne.

July 15

With Karl conveniently tending his estates, I meet the king in his private apartments at the palace. The moment he receives me he takes me into his arms, where I remain until the sun sets.

July 31

With Karl's return we must be circumspect. I send word to Lewis when Karl is occupied with the hope that Lewis is not. I try not to allow myself to think of what I do, but when I do think, I promise myself that I shall quit the king when I marry.

I truly shall, Marianne.

August 9

My romantic melodrama has been put on hold by another. Eugenie has broken with her Alessandro. Shaking with anger and face wet with tears, she told me she found her fiance *in flagrante delicto* with another woman, his landlady who Eugenie declares *ancien*, at least forty and *peu attrayant*. In a distraught mix of English and French, she described the scene to me with one uncomfortable detail after another, ending with Alessandro's claims that the affair meant nothing and that he loves only Eugenie. My dear friend confided that she will not marry him, saying that "if he acts so before the marriage, he will act far worse after."

August 11

I have just written Lewis, telling him I can see him no longer. I shall no longer risk what I have for what I cannot.

Weinheim, Wurttemberg
November 16

I am now Baroness Von Venningen. I was married today with my darling Babou in attendance, giving me away with tears in his eyes. His presence reassured me that my decision was the right one. Mama and Steely too attended. Their willingness to travel the distance from England meant much to me. I know my family approves of Karl and of our marriage. Surprisingly even the king sent his blessing with a handsome gift of crystal champagne flutes. Tomorrow we leave for Italy to bring home our son. A family complete.

I have finally accepted that my hopes for grand passion and adventure are the dreams of a foolish girl. I have a man who loves me. I am determined to love Karl as he deserves to be loved, Marianne.

My rebel heart will yield - at long last - to reason.

December 12

Since our return from Italy, my days are filled with the gentle pleasures of hearth and home. Karl has given me permission to redecorate the Weinheim estate as I see fit, and I am busy interviewing nurses for our Herberto who will be one year old next month. I see little of me in him, though he favors his father with his ginger hair and complexion. Bertie, as we call him, enjoys crawling after Tuilly, who runs circles around him. Karl can barely leave "his little man" out of his sight.

The isolation of our estate however is wearing upon me, all the more so since receiving an affectionate letter from Ludwig. He tells me about the continuing progress with the construction of his beloved Pinakothek and the crowning of his seventeen-year-old son Otto as King of Greece. Now he hopes to add to his collection of Grecian artifacts with his second son installed as Greece's head of state. He also asks after Karl and hopes that we are experiencing "the true companionship that marriage can offer," but also asks whether he might call upon me the next time I am at my home in Munich. He says that he misses "my lively spirit."

I miss his.

Munich, Bavaria

December 15

Under the pretense of shopping with Eugenie for purchases for our new home, I come to Munich to meet the king. Karl, happy in his role of new husband and father, suspects nothing. However Eugenie, who knows me better, discerns my true motivation and warns me "to take care."

I do *not* care. I have done as I was expected to do, but I shall do so no longer.

December 16

As I lay beside Lewis last night, I set to thinking about why we love or not, why - irrespective of looks, demeanor, or character - we love one but not another?

By any rational measure I should love Karl, but I do not. I love Lewis, but should not - an irrational love based upon want and need, not what should be. If I could, I would break my heart in two and give one half to each, but to do so my heart would stop beating. Instead, I give myself wholeheartedly without reason to one. I give my reasons - security, family, and home - to the other. How long I can, I do not know.

1834

Weinheim, Wurttemberg

January 3

I am two weeks late.

L fdqqrw eh vxuh zkhwkhu wkh idwkhu lv Nduo ru wkh nlqj.

February 5

I have told Karl that I am with child. He is delighted, naturally. I have written to family and friends - including the king - concerning the happy news.

March 2

Lewis has finally answered my letter. He sends his hearty congratulations to us both and tells me that my lovely presence at court will be missed.

Ambiguity - the quality of being open to more than one interpretation.

June 16

I am a nesting hen

Breeding discontent,

Ruminating

Over and

Over, waiting until I

Deliver - until I can fly.

August 18

My dear friend, I am afraid I have neglected you for far
too long.

My daughter was born just two days ago, an easy birth
followed by a difficult pregnancy - constant nausea
followed by swollen ankles, sleeplessness, and bouts of
dizziness were my lot for nine months. But now the
wretched business is over. I can look to the future,
whatever it may hold.

August 20

Karl is delighted with Berthe as we have named her. He
murmurs softly to her, taking care to support her head
as he cradles her in his arms. I tell him that I would like
to ask the king to be godfather to her. His quick
response surprises me, "Absolutely not, Jeanne." I do
not press him.

September 10

My confinement has finally ended. I had hoped to travel
soon to my home in Munich, and said as much to Karl.
He told me that he would not be able to spare the time

for a pleasure trip until later, after the autumn harvests on his estates. I replied that Eugenie and I would go alone. His reply? "I forbid you."

Kh nqrzv.

October 20

I have reconciled with my continued *confinement,* Marianne. I am a veritable *hausfrau.* I manage the household as chatelaine. I write letters to family and friends - including the king - telling them of the birth of my daughter. I entertain Karl's business associates, even his *dear* mother and sister whose lukewarm response to my efforts are a marked improvement to their earlier disdain. My only pleasures are letters from Lewis, though he nevers asks after Berthe.

It is a subject neither of us will broach.

Munich, Bavaria
November 25

Karl finally consented to spend the holidays in Munich. The long journey from Weinheim to the city was made even longer by two children and their nurses. But Karl is in a pleasant mood with a profitable year's work completed, and of course I am looking forward to holiday celebrations at the royal court.

December 6

The Von Venningens celebrated the beginning of Advent with *Sankt Nikolaus Tag*, or Saint Nicholas Day. In the German tradition good boys and girls place polished boots outside their bedroom doors in the hopes that Saint Nicholas will fill them with candy or small toys. Bad boys and girls however will receive only coal from *Knecht Ruprecht*, a frightful figure that only Germans could conjure. Fortunately, the saint's golden book recorded no naughty behavior from our Bertie and Berthe - though Karl and I, with the help of a mulled wine called *Gluhwein*, were decidedly so upon retiring to our bed chamber.

December 15

My husband and I stroll the market of Munich which is decorated with hundreds of candles and yards upon yards of greenery for the holidays. Vendors shout to us, asking that we come look at their holiday wares. Intricate wooden toys and painted Christmas ornaments. Christmas *stollen* and gingerbread men. Children sing carols for *pfenninge* which they use to buy *plaetzchen*, a popular Christmas cookie. We watch skaters cut figures upon the ice of the *Feldmochinger See*, while eating *knackwurst* and drinking Bavarian beer. A gentle snowfall dusts the streets as we make our way back to our carriage and onward home.

Tomorrow we attend the Christmas ball at court. I shall see my king again.

December 17

A night of light and luminaries. Under gaslight chandeliers Munich society meets to gossip, dance, and celebrate the holiday season.

It had been years since I had danced the night, but I have not forgotten how. The dances of my youth - quadrille, reel, waltz, and polonaise - quickly come back to me. Did I just write *my youth*? At twenty-seven I am hardly old - especially when dancing! I must have taken a turn about the floor with nearly every man present, even my reluctant husband. But I remember only one. As Lewis took me in his arms, we exchanged pleasantries until he asked me *sotto voce*, "Affectionate letters, stolen glances, and Austrian waltzes are not enough, my Ianthe. When will we meet again?"

We agreed to the day after next at his beloved museum, Alte Pinakothek.

December 20

Yesterday under the pretense of Christmas shopping with Eugenie, we met.

Amidst the debris of construction we make our way to the small living space created for him by his workers, now on holiday leave. A stool, a small wood stove, nightstand, and canopied bed are its only furnishings. I watch as he quickly builds a fire. I remark on his skill with the task and remind him of the fires he tended at the hunting lodge at Jagdschloss, where we first made love. "We have history, my dear," he remarks. "Let us begin our future," I answer.

We do - with hands, lips, and bodies joined.

Later, I awake to a painting displayed before me. "She is called *Sleeping Venus*, painted by the great Titian," says Lewis. "She is one of my favorites, but you are more lovely than she."

He thinks me lovely. I would prefer to be loved.

1835

Munich, Bavaria

January 1

New Year's Day. We return to Weinheim tomorrow.

I dread the coming winter.

Weinheim, Wurttemberg

February 2

Candlemas. I remember my grandfather taking the household candles to the local church to be blessed in honor of the presentation of the infant Jesus at the Temple in Jerusalem. I see Candlemas as winter's center, a day when spring can only be envisioned. The days now are noticeably longer, the path of the sun higher, but the cold will not release its grip upon the sleeping land.

Our home is drafty and dry, the only warmth found by the hearth, where the children play with a humming top. Karl drafts plans for a spring planting of grapevines on one of the southern estates, while I pluck my guitar listlessly and think of Munich.

March 1

I have written the king two times since the holidays and have received no response. Whatever could be wrong, Marianne?

Munich, Bavaria

April 3

Karl has treated me with a trip to the city just in time for my birthday and the spring social season. I am determined to enjoy myself despite the king's neglect of me.

I have met the most amusing man, Honore de Balzac. Perhaps you have heard of him? He is a French novelist and playwright. Jovial, ambitious, and boastful he is also a man of many words, both written and not. Even I, who can typically banter with the best, find it difficult to follow the rush of thoughts he issues. Monsieur Balzac speaks of industrial enterprise, political intrigue, romantic love, social scandals, and the worlds of art and literature with equal gusto. Yet he listens attentively when I speak of my past. I have been told that many aristocratic women, despite his homeliness, have taken him as a lover.

Shame on you, Marianne. I know what you are thinking - but I assure you my interest in him is strictly platonic.

April 7

I have asked Karl whether we might invite Monsieur Balzac to Weinheim. He has agreed. Karl enjoys the company of my new acquaintance almost as much as I do.

I still have not seen nor heard from Lewis.

Weinheim, Wurttemberg
May 20

Monsieur Balzac finally paid call en route to his beloved Paris. We again became immediate confidants. Over a typically British tea with scones and clotted cream, we spoke of my "remarkable career" as he deemed it, as well as his affair with a Polish countess, Eveline Hanska, who he hopes to marry one day. Our conversation then turned to his recently published novel, *Le Pere Goriot*, which I had just finished reading. In it he examines the struggles of individuals who seek, sometimes ruthlessly, greater social status.

"Are you familiar with such individuals, Baroness?" he asked me.

"Of course. Most of London society seeks such advancement."

"And what do you seek?"

"I seek only love and freedom, Monsieur."

"Only? Can one really have both?"

Regrettably, our conversation was interrupted by Karl for a tour of the grounds, where we spoke of matters far more practical, but far less significant.

May 21

Monsieur Balzac has departed, but my mind returns to his questions of me. I do fear that what I seek does not exist.

June 5

Lewis has finally written, apologizing for his silence. He tells me that he has been quite ill, but asks to see me.

I must go to him, Marianne.

June 7

I first thought to flee Weinheim without telling Karl, but my sense of decency prevailed. I faced him with my intent to leave for Munich, for a short stay, I assured him.

"No, you will not, Jeanne."

I shall wait until he leaves next week for his southern estate, coward that I am.

June 10

Last night I had a strange dream. Like most dreams its sequence was fragmented. Images strung together to create impressions with meaning perhaps, though little form.

In it I walk through Forston, my family home. Through a hallway I do not recognize, I try one door after another. The first two are locked. The third opens to reveal Karl, Herberto, and Berthe sitting together before a fire. They do not acknowledge me, and I quietly close the door. I move on to open the next door which reveals Lewis and a striking brunette in an embrace. They see me and laugh, sending me down the hallway to escape the sound. I then try to open subsequent doors, rattling each latch in an attempt to unlock them - without success.

Next I find myself in moonlight with no discernible landmarks. Clad only in my shift, I begin walking without direction or destination. Suddenly I hear a soft whinny in the distance. "Mazeppa?" I ask. He appears suddenly before me, pawing at the earth, demanding, as he will, to ride with me. I mount him without saddle or stirrups and cling to his mane as we ride east toward the ever-rising moon.

June 15

My dear Karl,

Although I have written my share of difficult letters, I have written no letter more difficult than this.

I have tried, but I can try no longer. Each day I grow more unhappy for no other reason than I am. You see, I am terribly flawed, my darling. I do not love those I should and love those I should not.

In novels that I have read when one lover breaks with another, the one who breaks will inevitably tell the one broken, "You deserve better than I." I always thought such declarations false, words found only in fiction. But I was wrong. The books were true. You *do* deserve one better than I, Karl.

You must let me go.

Jeanne

June 16

Before first light Eugenie and I depart by hired coach for my home in Munich.

Munich, Bavaria

June 19

We have arrived. I wasted no time in writing to Lewis, telling him that I have returned to the city, eager to see him.

June 21

I have just returned from seeing Lewis. He is much changed. The passionate and driven king I have loved has vanished. In his place is an aging man, thin and pale with trembling hands. I asked the nature of his illness. He replied that after the holidays he suffered a melancholy so severe that he struggled to even rise from his bed. He revealed that he had experienced previous melancholic bouts, but none so intense. He feared he might go mad. Only with the approach of spring did he slowly regain his wits and fight the despair claiming him.

I have resolved to see him, and write to him, every day.
He will not fight alone.

June 25

Each day I pay a call to the king at his apartments in
Nymphenburg Castle by the private entrance. I bring
small gifts - sweet wine, dark chocolates, or rambling
roses from my garden. I do not stay long, and there is
no physical intimacy between us with the exception of
his kiss of my hand in welcome, my kiss on his cheek in
farewell. We talk as we once did.

I send short notes to him each day. Sometimes I write
in the Caesar cipher that I shared with my brothers so
many years ago and still share with you, sometimes I
write in verse. Other times I ask him questions of a
metaphysical nature. Do animals have souls? Do
humans have free will? Why do we dream?

He responds to each question I pose, sometimes in
cipher or in verse with each line ending in rhyming
couplets.

His health improves a little each day, though his
rhymes do not.

June 27

As I knew he would, Karl has followed me to Munich. He demands that I return with him to Weinheim and admonishes me for leaving the children with the servants, while I meet with the king.

I refuse to return.

June 28

Although I have never known Karl to resort to force, I have nevertheless taken precautions. I have hired a locksmith to change every lock on my estate. When I visit Lewis I make sure that my driver takes the carriage through a circuitous route to the palace, in the fear that Karl may follow.

July 10

After repeated efforts to persuade me to return home, Karl has finally accepted, albeit begrudgingly, my move here - though he refuses to speak of any end to our marriage when I broach the subject. Since I cannot stomach another quarrel, I do not press the issue.

July 30

My life is again mine. I drink my freedom like a drunkard drinks port. I am intoxicated by the simplest pleasures - riding a much neglected Mazeppa, strolling my grounds with Eugenie and Tuilly, visiting Lewis who regals me with his latest project, his illness now forgotten in a new manic display of energy.

Now I must look to my future.

August 12

My dear Lewis seeing my growing restlessness, proposed a most interesting proposition the other day. He suggested that I might lead my own *salon* with his patronage. I am familiar enough with these gatherings having attended the salon of Princess Belgiojoso, who entertained prominent intellectuals and *artistes* during my time in Paris. I have also established a circle of like-minded friends from my time spent at Tambosi's. And of course I long for more stimulating conversation since leaving Weinheim and returning to Munich.

I believe I shall take my king's suggestion, Marianne.

September 10

I have spent the last month in a fury of activity with my pursuit of a "bluestocking" career. First, I wrote invitations to my first *soiree*, asking men and women of my acquaintance who can amuse and be amused, regardless of their social rank, to attend. While I wrote until my hand cramped, I ordered a thorough cleaning of the house with Eugenie's supervision. Second, I procured the finest varieties of coffee and tea and asked Cook to create assorted nibbles for the occasion: cold meats and cheeses and her signature custard tarts. Finally I, with the King's assistance, decided upon nimble topics for discussion during the evening.

I just had a disturbing thought, Marianne. Looking at my description of my meticulous party design, I am beginning to sound suspiciously like my mother.

Mein Gott.

September 20

Last night was a success. Resoundingly so? Perhaps not, but companionship and inventive discourse was had by all but one. My right arm, Eugenie, fell ill with a chill serious enough that I suggested she retire before the first guest arrived, a suggestion she accepted gratefully.

I now had to face the evening alone and with some trepidation. That is until the king arrived before any other guests. By decree, he asked the servants to set the sideboards with food and drink, while we lighted candles and placed flower arrangements. My disheveled but courtly Lewis then acted as doorman to my surprised and delighted guests. Soon all invited had arrived.

We listened to young Josephine Lang who sang and played piano beautifully. She is so talented that she has attracted the attention of the great composer, Schumann and of Mendelssohn whose song, *Auf Flügeln des Gesanges*, or *On Wings of Song*, she performed for us. The poet who wrote the lyrics to the piece, Heinrich Heine, then recited some of his short poems including my favorite, *A Palm Tree*:

A single fir-tree, lonely,
on a northern mountain height,
sleeps in a white blanket,
draped in snow and ice.

His dreams are of a palm-tree,
who, far in eastern lands,
weeps, alone and silent,
among the burning sands.

Heinrich, I learned from Lewis, is part of the *Young Germany* movement which espouses liberal political ideas. Fortunately, I had the foresight to declare to my guests that my salon has only one rule: political discourse is banned. Instead we spoke of concerns far from the realities of state. We discussed two questions: Should art be beautiful? And, can men and women be lovers *and* friends? No consensus for either was found among my guests, though the questions did provide much amusement.

Lewis spends the night. In my bed we prove - at least to each other - that men and women can indeed be both lovers and friends.

October 5

Karl has brought the children to Munich for a visit. They have grown much in the few months since I last saw them. Bertie is quite the little man and resembles his father more and more with his fair skin and russet hair. Bertha too has grown and is now walking so well that she follows poor Tuilly everywhere, pulling his hair with hands sticky with jam. Karl meanwhile watches my every move and asks whether he and the children might spend the night. I agree.

Was it Shakespeare that said, "Absence makes the heart grow fonder?"

Are you shocked that I sleep with the king *and* my husband, Marianne? Zhoo, dw ohdvw L gr qrw gr vr frqfxuuhqwob, pb ghdu!

October 20

My second soiree went swimmingly, though Lewis was unable to attend. Though I missed his company, I managed quite well without him. In fact, the conversation was decidedly more casual without his royal presence and the more formal entertainment offered in our previous meeting. I played the guitar and lute to accompany an old acquaintance from Paris, a young Frenchman named Philippe, who flirted most charmingly with Eugenie during our duets. I was so glad to see that she returned his interest, since she has been without male companionship since her break with Alessandro.

During the evening as we spoke of the latest novels, I learned that Balzac has written another book called *Le Lys dans la Vallée* and, rumor has it, he claims that one of its characters, an Arabella Dudley, is modelled after me. My curiosity of course demands that I locate a copy.

November 10

My copy of *The Lily in the Valley* finally arrived from a Paris bookseller yesterday. I spent disagreeable hours reading it, Marianne.

The novella is in the form of a confession of a young Frenchman named *Felix* de Vandenesse who writes to his fiancee, Natalie, about his past love affairs - one with the saintly Henriette de Mortsauf and another with the sinning Arabella Dudley.

I realize that authors must take a certain measure of artistic license in the development of their characters, but if Monsieur Balzac used me as inspiration for his Arabella Dudley, I fail to see the resemblance. She is described as having "an iron nature" and being "so strong that she fears no struggle." Furthermore, the author slanders all British females by saying, "the tongue of an Englishwoman is like that of a tiger tearing the flesh from the bone" and that she "opens and shuts her heart with the ease of a British mechanism."

Telle merde! Monsieur Balzac obviously knows little about British women, in general, and me, specifically. And his protagonist is most insufferable! I doubt that I can force myself to complete the book.

November 11

Perhaps I was hasty in my judgment of *The Lily in the Valley*. I *did* complete it and found the ending surprising and quite clever. In it the author finishes his story with Felix de Vandenesse receiving a reply to his confession from his Natalie. In her response she breaks off her engagement with him, citing his indiscretion in writing about old lovers to a new one and his failure to understand the very nature of women, both saintly and sinning. It would seem Felix's narration is not to be trusted, Marianne.

Clearly Monsieur Balzac knows more about the nature of women *and* the intricacies of love than I first thought!

Weinheim, Wurttemberg

December 2

I have joined the family for Advent. I feel as though I lead a double life, one in Munich, another here in Weinheim. And with that double life I am two women, Baroness Von Venningen, a wife and mother, with a *Doppelganger* who is neither, who is simply Jane Digby.

Now roles reverse. A twin stranger enjoys the pleasures of home, a doting husband who plays spillikins with our beautiful children. We all laugh as he tries to remove one of the straws without disturbing the others and fails.

Meanwhile, Jane Digby longs for Munich - and more.

1836

Munich, Bavaria

January 6

With Christmas gone so has the cold weather. Munich is experiencing a *foehn* wind, warm and dry, that blows from the Alpine slopes. I am told they cause headaches and moodiness in many people. Fortunately I am not one. I am enjoying the balmy temperatures and hope they remain until at least tomorrow for my first salon of the new year, a costume party to which I invited old friends from Tambosi's. Philippe, Eugenie's new beau, asked whether a young nobleman from the Greek embassy might also attend. I, of course, said yes. The more the merrier.

January 8

Last night I fell in love. Instantly. Madly. Completely.

A Greek count appeared at my door in his country's costume: a pleated white smock decorated with colorful scarves and embroidered panels. Cinched at the waist with gold braid, the smock fell to knee length, revealing handsome calves encased in silk stocking and large feet in patent leather. No sooner had I taken in this vision of male splendor than I heard his deep voice in strongly accented, though perfect, English ask whether I was Baroness Von Venningen. I looked up to see the beautiful face of a young man with great moustaches and sideburns and a head of thick black hair barely contained by a red velvet cap and tassel. After I replied in the affirmative, he smiled and bowed deeply, saying, "My name is Spiridon Theotoky. I was told you were expecting me."

He did not leave my side the whole evening. He spoke of his home in Corfu, an island off the coast of Greece. It is named, he told me, after a beautiful nymph who Poseidon fell in love with and abducted. Located on the Ionian sea, Corfu is one of its largest islands, consisting of rugged mountains and pebble beaches. Spiros, as he insisted I call him, asked whether I had ever travelled to his island. I replied that I had never visited Greece, though I hoped to. "Perhaps, we might see it together some day," he whispered.

Later, we took advantage of the mild evening and repaired to the veranda. There I pointed out the constellation Cassiopeia, whose stars formed a lazy W to our south. "You are more beautiful than she," he told me. I turned to him, and he gathered me into his arms and kissed me - gently, at first.

January 9

He left reluctantly last night, as I remembered my duties as hostess. I thanked my guests and bid them farewell - all the while wishing they would disappear, that the world would disappear, so that Spiros and I could have the world without them.

Now I wait for him. We are to meet at eleven. It is now ten, but still I peer out my front windows hoping that he will arrive early, as eager as I am.

He does. He is. He stands by the chestnut tree.

January 10

I ran down the stairs as quickly as my skirts would allow me, pausing to catch my breath before I opened the door. I called out to him, and he strode across the lawn, now brown with winter. "Jane," he said as he came to me. I said nothing in return. Instead I reached for his hand and led him straight away to my bedchamber, where we undressed as quickly as our trembling hands would allow us. When I looked at him naked, so young and without blemish, I worried about the years between us and my own body, stretched and pulled by the birth of four children. But the look in his eyes assured me that he saw me as I saw him - as perfect as new lovers do.

"I cannot wait," he said. "Neither can I," I answered. We loved *allegro* - joyful, lively, and fast.

Later we loved *adagio*. Our hands and lips slowly explored our flesh, whilst we softly joined again.

January 15

He arrives each day at the same time. Some days we spend in bed, others we explore the countryside of Munich by sleigh. The foehn winds have left us, replaced by cold temperatures and a thick blanket of snow. Accustomed to the hot climate of Greece, Spiros is smitten by our Bavarian winter.

Today, in addition to sleighing, we skate on a nearby pond, borrowing homemade skates from local children who laugh at our graceless attempts to glide upon the ice. Later we return to my home for mugs of hot cocoa and talk for hours before a warm fire until it is time for bed, where we talk no more.

January 30

Today is the first day I have not awaited the arrival of my count. Instead, I attend the grand opening of King Ludwig's beloved Pinakothek. And although I am happy for my friend's success and proud of his achievement in finally completing what will likely be the most significant art museum on the continent, I am eager to return home so that I might see Spiros. I even go so far as to feign illness when Lewis asks to meet with me later. It is the first time I ever lied to him, Marianne.

February 1

I received two letters this morning. The first was from Lewis asking after my health and asking when we might meet again. As I opened the next letter, I thought about how I might decline his invitation without revealing my affair with the count. However upon reading the second letter, that thought quickly became inconsequential.

The letter was from my husband. He has learned of my affair with Spiros.

The Road to Heidelberg
February 2

Soon after I read Karl's letter, Spiros arrived for our morning liaison. I explained to him that my husband knew of our affair - and that he was now on his way to Munich. Spiros immediately suggested that we elope - which is how I find myself now, only hours later, on the road to Heidelberg with my dearest love, pursuing our freedom.

Are we not mad, Marianne?

Weinheim, Wurttemberg
February 4

We were only a few miles from our destination, an inn near Heidelberg University where Spiros planned to spend the night, when my husband found us. He had learned from Eugenie, who remained behind in Munich, the road which we travelled. He had spent day and night upon my gelding, Mazeppa, with only a pair of heirloom dueling pistols in his possession.

Karl rode furiously beside our carriage, while I urged the coachmen to pick up speed to outpace him, but they declined, citing the health of their horses and their own safety. As the carriage slowed, I then pleaded with Spiros to allow me to speak to my husband, to reason with him the best I could. He refused. "I am no coward," he said. He kissed me quickly and told me to stay in the carriage before exiting to face my husband. Soon however the sound of angry male voices forced me to follow my lover into the dark German night. There I found Karl and Spiros face-to-face as my husband declared, "You have played me false, sir. I shall have my satisfaction." He then turned to me and added, "My happiness has ended."

The two men then coolly decided upon the rules of engagement. No seconds, as the coachmen were emphatically disinclined to intervene. The combatants agreed that the duel would be fought to first blood and at twenty paces with Karl giving Spiros first shot. After glancing at me briefly, Spiros told my husband that there had never been more than a "deep and sincere friendship" between us. My husband accepted his lie graciously, as he prepared the weapons.

Twenty paces takes longer to walk than one might imagine, Marianne. With only moonlight to see by, I watched as they counted their paces and stood facing each other. Spiros then raised his arm, cocked his pistol and aimed. A bright flash. A resounding shot. The smell of sulfur. Karl stood, unharmed.

I knew Karl would unlikely miss his target. My knowledge proved right. Spiros fell to the ground, bleeding from a shot somewhere near his left breast. I ran to him and I too fell to the ground before him, searching for the wound amid his blood. I found it, well above his heart to my relief. As I attempted to stanch the wound with my gloved hands, I called for Karl. He came to me, white and visibly shaken. I asked that the unconscious Spiros be taken to the carriage and onward to Heidelberg where we might find a doctor to tend to my lover's wound. Karl agreed, ordering the coachmen to carry him to the carriage.

At Heidelberg Karl procured a doctor, an old professor from his days at the university. With a reassuring proficiency Dr. Gottfried removed the bullet and dressed Spiro's wound, remarking that had the bullet been an inch closer to his heart, he would surely have died. Even so, with the loss of blood and the risk of infection, Spiros might need weeks to recuperate. Karl insisted that we take him to our home in Weinheim, little more than ten miles away.

How could I argue?

February 10

I prove a capable nurse. And a single bullet proves unequal to my lover's youth and stamina. He is already well enough to complain of his bed rest and worries about the strange situation in which we find ourselves.

Karl has spoken nothing about the events of the past week and nothing about the future. It is his silence that worries me.

February 12

My husband has asked me for a year to repair our marriage - a year until I decide my future - though Karl demands that I neither see nor write my lover until then.

I agree, though reluctantly. I owe Karl that much.

February 14

Today I completed two very difficult tasks. First, I wrote to the king, telling him of the dramatic events that have transpired. I doubt that he will ever forgive me and suspect I will lose his friendship forever.

Second, I said my goodbyes to Spiros who, though unhappy with the separation that my husband demands of us, nevertheless concedes that it is *my* decision to make for the both of us. I cried most desperately as he left for the Greek embassy in Munich where he will continue his convalescence. Before he entered the carriage, he gave me a swift kiss upon the cheek and whispered, "I will not forget you." He then shook hands with the man who nearly killed him ten days ago. How strange is the gentleman's code of honour.

I really think men much simpler creatures than women, Marianne.

March 1

The past two weeks Karl and I have established an uneasy truce. He suggests that I visit my family in England with Eugenie and the children, while he conducts business with his estates. I agree, though I suspect his suggestion betrays his fear that I might flee to Spiros with his absence if I remain here.

His fear is not unfounded.

Forston House
Dorset, England
March 20

Why is it that I still consider Dorset home, despite the years I have spent elsewhere? Nowhere else have the skies been greyer, the grass greener, the hedgerows tidier, or the sheep fatter. I have seen great cities and have been stirred by their bustle and swagger, but the quiet hamlets and pasture of Dorset curl round my heart anew as we make our way to Forston.

The first person I see is Kenelm standing by the brick fence which surrounds our childhood home. I scarcely recognize him. Has it really been over five years since I last saw my baby brother? He is now a man of twenty-five and Vicar of Tattershall. "Jane," he shouts upon seeing us exit the coach. Unusually shy, Herberto and Berthe hide behind Eugenie's skirts, while Kenhelm greets me with a warm hug as I brush tears from my eyes. "You are as beautiful as I remember. They're all waiting for you inside." *All* includes Steely, her sister, Jane, Jane's husband, Kenelm's fiancee, Emily, Auntie Anne - and, of course, Mama and Papa.

I am home.

March 24

Herberto and Berthe bask in familial affection, as do I - so much so that I delay telling my family about the latest scandal associated with me. I know that I must, since such stories spread quickly, even to remote Dorset.

Mama and Papa deserve to hear of my latest scrape from me, though I know the hearing will distress them.

April 3

Today, on my twenty-ninth birthday, I told my parents about my affair with Spiros and the duel for my affection, as well as the year long *stay* Karl demanded.

My news was not well-received.

Papa was the first to speak. "I did not know you were unhappy, Jane." La Madre seized on the word. "*Unhappy*? Why should happiness be the matter? Jane is a grown woman with a husband, children, and social position. Should she toss them all away because she thinks herself unhappy?" I replied that my unhappiness is a *matter* to me, but she dismissed my answer with a cutting rebuke. "My father and your brother, Edward have refused to call on us during your visit, seeing how your first marriage ended. Now you are considering ending the second in the same manner?"

"Yes," I whispered. Without a word, Mama stood and with a final scowl left the room.

"She is right, you know," my father said, before he too left me.

April 4

Aunt Anne paid Forston another call today. I walked the gardens with her, as we enjoyed the first bloom of spring. Before we made our way inside, she told me that Mama had told her of my *dilemma.* "I suppose you think as they do, that I should remain with my husband."

"Not at all. I have always believed a woman must look to her happiness, since the world certainly will not."

May 20

I say farewell to my family tomorrow. I foolishly thought my visit home would help me make my decision, but it has only complicated it. I cannot find the answers for my future in the past.

Weinheim, Württemberg

July 12

I mark time. Six more months. I write again to the king, but he does not reply. I worry that Spiros has forgotten me, as any young man might. I find fault with Karl and the children, though they are faultless.

It is *my* fault for agreeing to this charade.

1837

Weinheim, Württemberg

January 1

Less than six weeks.

February 13

I have received word from my Spiros. As I tear open the letter and read the short message, the postboy stands ready for my reply.

My dearest Jane,

I have kept my word to the day, though I cannot wait a day longer. I am staying in a cottage beside the *Goldener Pflug* near Weinheim. I impatiently await your reply.

Se agapo,
S.

I give swift reply:

My darling, you have not forgotten me! I will fly to you tomorrow by twelve noon. I count the hours, the minutes.

Until then,
J.

February 14

I rode at noon as I do most everyday, but today my destination was clear.

I hack through the cold woods urging Mazeppa from trot to canter to gallop, heedless of frozen ground and stream. I look only forward, as his ears move back and forth with each stride we take. Finally we arrive on the *Bergstrasse*, the ancient mountain road to Weinheim where, if memory serves me right, the inn lies less than two miles away. We press on until I see the inn's red tile roof. I ease our pace, looking for the cottage Spiros has taken. When I spot a small timber-framed structure, I dismount and tie Mazeppa to the hitch post. I then knock on the door, suddenly nervous at my boldness.

Only seconds later, Spiros opens the door and quickly pulls me inside. Holding my face in his hands, he looks at me with such love in his eyes that I begin to cry and whisper, "I thought you had forgotten me." As he wipes the tears from my eyes, he replies, "Never."

We recall each kiss and each touch, remembering the taste and feel of the other. With each heavy breath we recount our love, thrust by thrust by thrust - until we lie warm, spent by our efforts.

"You will never send me away again," he says softly.

"Never again."

February 20

We meet secretly each afternoon. Sometimes afternoons are not enough. Then I steal away from home, riding Mazeppa into the dark and cold of night until I am made warm again by my lover's touch.

I do not tell Karl of Spiro's return, Marianne. Perhaps I fear the recriminations sure to ensue, or perhaps I crave the intrigue of an illicit rendezvous - a secret that sweetens my imperturbable life of late. Perhaps I still need my husband and children, as they need me.

Each time I leave the arms of Spiros, he asks that we elope once again. I tell him to be patient until I can tell Karl that our marriage is over, knowing each time that I should postpone no longer.

Nevertheless, I do.

The Road to Paris
March 1

We fled last night. Our destination lies over three hundred miles away. I hope the miles are enough. We left with barely more than the clothes on our backs and told no one of our plans, even Eugenie has been left behind and without word of our departure. With the exception of each other, we trust no one.

Paris, France
March 6

We have arrived safely in Paris. Though we are currently staying at *Le Meurice*, our finances demand that we find more affordable accommodations outside the city. I am meeting today with my banker, Monsieur Armel, to request an advance upon my monthly allowance from my first marriage and to initiate the sale of my home in Munich.

The bridges are burned.

March 8

With an advance secured, Spiros and I have leased a small house as Mr. and Mrs. Pappas, the name a nod to my old friend Andriana from the Tunbridge Wells School for Young Ladies. We bask in the pleasures of our home and the intimacy of our feigned marriage, though we both realize that the pretense may be shattered by reality. As we well know, my husband will not forfeit me without a struggle.

March 20

Reality has found us more quickly than I thought possible, thanks to the underhanded efforts of Monsieur Armel who wrote to my husband concerning my business dealings here in Paris. Fortunately Karl arrived at our home when Spiros was in *Marseille* conducting his own business concerns, making the scene an ugly duel of words with me and me only. His first strike began with his assertion that he could have me returned to Wurttemberg since German law demands that a wife have her husband's permission to leave the country. I parried this assertion with the declaration that "no man will hold me prisoner" and that "I would flee again at the earliest opportunity." To which he retorted, "I should have never married you, knowing your reputation." I reminded him that I never wanted to marry him and asserted truthfully and most cruelly that I *never* loved him. Lastly, I told him that I required a divorce.

First blood was mine.

March 22

My cruel words did indeed find their mark, but the blow was not fatal, as Karl's letter, included here, demonstrates:

My dearest Jeanne,

I much regret my harsh words during our last meeting. Believe me when I tell you that those words were borne from the pain of loving you and from the anger that you do not return that love. I shall never, never regret marrying you.

Nevertheless, I must look to my future and the future of our children. I shall grant you the divorce you seek, though only after we have lived apart for one year's time. I still hope, perhaps foolishly, that your, or his, passion will fade, and that you will return to us.

Faithfully yours,

Karl

He stalls for time once again. And once again, I have no choice but to acquiesce to his decision, if I wish to remarry.

Marseille, France

April 4

We are married. Let me explain.

Just when I thought Spiros was reconciled to the year's
wait, he prepared the means for our marriage on my
thirtieth birthday - a clandestine marriage with our
vows spoken privately before a witness, a fellow
countryman, a Mr. Constantine, who also manages his
business affairs here in Marseille.

How could I not be pleased by such a romantic gesture?
And although our secret marriage is not genuine by the
standards society demands, our love will nevertheless
withstand the time demanded - of that I am certain.
Until then our secret will remain ours alone.

April 5

We are spending a short *honeymoon* here in Marseille. Spiros considers the city a second home with its large numbers of Grecian citizens. The city, according to Spiros, was founded by the Greeks thousands of years ago, though it was later conquered by Rome and Julius Caesar, and even later became a center for early Christianity. In modern times, the city was a hub for the French Revolution and the source of France's national anthem, *La Marseillaise*. I tease Spiros about his history lesson, telling him that he should become a lecturer at the *Sorbonne*. He replies that most Greeks know history, especially ancient history, as I will learn when we make our home there.

"When we make our home there." I will dream on that thought, but for now I am content to explore the streets of Marseille and to enjoy the Mediterranean salt air with my love by my side.

Paris, France

April 30

Karl writes me from Weinheim in reply to a letter I sent a week ago, in which I asked after the children, Tuilly, and Mazeppa. I also requested that Eugenie, having broken with her Philippe, be sent to Paris to me, if she is so inclined. He tells me that the Herberto and Berthe are well, though "they miss their little mother" and that little Tuilly is a comfort to them. He will also make sure that Mazeppa is given the care such "a noble steed" deserves. Eugenie, he says, is eager to return to me and should arrive in Paris shortly.

He also forwarded a letter from King Ludwig.

May 1

I have managed to forget the letter from Lewis for nearly a day. It lie unopened on my *secretaire* until just a few moments ago:

Ianthe,

I am deeply troubled by the events you described in your last letter, as well as the latest, and most relentless, gossip we in Bavaria hear about the notorious Baroness Von Venningen. Your conduct wounds me, so much so that I can scarcely write. Perhaps it is best for all that we write no more. Nonetheless, I shall always wish you happiness.

Basily

I replied, though I fear my letter will do little to mend our friendship:

My dear Basily,

Please forgive me my rash actions of late. I assure you that those actions were not conducted by any meanness of spirit, but rather by my pursuit of freedom and passion, those very pursuits that you urged me to embrace so many years ago. I am what I am - desperately flawed, but still desiring Your Majesty's friendship.

Yours always,

Ianthe

May 17

Eugenie returned to me a few days ago. I thought she
would be eager to live once again in Paris, her former
home. I even thought she would be eager to see me,
since our relationship is one more of friendship than of
mistress and servant. But her peculiar moodiness
persisted for so long that it caused me to ask what was
the matter. She immediately burst into tears at the
question, telling me that my husband had asked her to
report to him concerning the state of my relations with
Spiros who he suspected was a "fortune hunter." This
request was only the last of many. During the course of
our marriage he would often ask her to look at my
diary entries and report any "unseemly" remarks.

"Why would you agree to such a thing, Eugenie?" I
asked angrily.

"I thought my position was at stake, my lady."

Her unexpected confession reminded me of an incident
years ago during my first marriage when you - my dear

Marianne - went missing, only to reappear under puzzling circumstances.

"Did you also report to Lord Ellenborough in such a manner?" I asked.

"Yes," she replied bursting into tears once again. "He said that I must - or that he would have me dismissed."

With that, my anger at her turned to my husbands, who had not only intruded upon my most private thoughts but also had enlisted the help of my vulnerable friend to do so. Their betrayals sting, yet it is pointless to pursue the matter. I do, however, regret much less my treatment of both men.

Fortune-hunter, indeed!

May 18

I have asked Eugenie to remain in my employment, though I demanded that she never keep such secrets from me again. She gratefully agreed.

No word from Lewis.

June 21

The news travelled quickly across the Channel. King William IV has died. His eighteen-year-old niece, Victoria, has been declared Queen of England.

Long live the Queen.

July 20

Mama writes with good news. Grandfather has, after *six* offers, finally accepted a peerage from the new Queen. He is now the 1st Earl of Leicester. The title, of course, delights my socially astute mother, and, I am sure, his wife and children, though I doubt Grandpapa takes much pleasure in it, having once called the House of Lords, "the hospital for incurables."

Still no word from Lewis. I suppose I should not be surprised that our last chapter has been written. I must learn to accept that our friendship has ended.

August 13

Today I learned to appreciate Paris again, arm-in-arm with my Spiros.

My painful past here had made me uncharacteristically reclusive, avoiding the great city's hubbub and history - that is until Spiros insisted that I act as his guide this bright summer day.

With France's "citizen king," Louis Philippe, now ruling the country after the tumultuous years of Napoleon and the 1830 revolution, Paris has experienced an enthusiastic revival. Renovations to Notre-Dame cathedral are reportedly being discussed, spurred by the popularity of Victor Hugo's novels. The Louvre too is adding to its collections, as I learned when we toured both old and new school paintings.

Yet simply walking the streets of Paris this Sunday was more buoyant to my spirits than any ancient chapel or fine museum. We walked to the Champ-Elysees where the *bourgeois* amused themselves and their children in seeing the exhibits of mountebanks, *grimaciers*, and rope walkers. We proceeded to the Tuileries garden where Parisians sat on benches under majestic trees conversing or reading newspapers while sipping lemonade or coffee. We crossed over the Pont de l'Ecole where scores of washerwomen, mindless of the rest day, beat dirty linens clean.

May Paris always be so alive, Marianne.

September 1

Both Spiros and I grow impatient with our state of limbo. We count the days until March 22, the date when Karl indicated he would initiate our divorce. I had hoped that I might become pregnant, so that Karl would see the futility of his postponement, but alas, despite our frequent attempts to conceive, my relentless fruitfulness has abandoned me when I need it the most.

Nevertheless, we take great pleasure in our persistence.

October 15

As the first leaves of autumn fall Spiros and I visit Paris's famous Diorama created by Charles Bouton and Louis Daguerre. We, with some three hundred other patrons, rotated on a massive turnstile viewing two landscapes: France's village of Thiers and Switzerland's valley of Sarnen. With a sleight of hand on a prodigious scale, village and valley came to life. I could swear we were witnessing natural settings. Thiers appeared, first in brilliant sunshine until the scene slowly darkened to moonlit sky. Sarnen similarly changed from summer meadow to snow laden field. Each transformation was accompanied by gasps from the audience who were as astounded as Spiros and I. Our perceptions deceived us into thinking an imitation of reality was something true.

As we departed I heard someone whisper that Monsieur Daguerre is perfecting an even more astounding process in which images on silver plate will create faithful representations of both landscapes *and* portraits. Now what terrific magic that would be, Marianne!

November 19

My dear Steely has been sending me monthly installments of a new book that is all the rage in London, Charles Dickens's *Oliver Twist*. I have taken the precaution of reading the installments *before* her letters, since my former governess's enthusiasm often causes her to divulge crucial details of plot that I would really prefer to discover myself! Nevertheless, my new correspondence with her fills the long hours of Spiros's absence. He returned to Greece last month upon learning of the death of his grandmother and will not return to me until Yuletide.

"I am to wait, though waiting so be hell."

December 22

William Shakespeare thought waiting hell, but the end of waiting is like heaven, as I discovered yesterday with Spiros's return:

I had fallen asleep by the fire - having just finished Chapter Nineteen of *Oliver Twist* in which wily Fagin enlists innocent Oliver's help with a housebreaking - when I was gently awakened by a soft touch upon my face. I opened my eyes to the gentle smile of my Spiros who placed his fingers on my lips and whispered, "No words." I followed him into the bedchamber where only the exhale of gaslight broke the silence. By its soft glow I watched as Spiros discarded his clothes piece by piece until his naked body shone bronze. I then discarded my dressing gown and night shift before I slipped under the bed covers. "I'm cold," I complained. "I, too," he replied, as he joined me under the covers where we soon were cold no longer.

December 25

In preparation for our exchange of Christmas gifts, I had taken note of anything that caught my lover's eye during our many excursions to the Passage des Panoramas. I decided upon a three-piece silver toilet set and a Saint-Louis paperweight made of lead crystal as my gifts to him. I also included a self-portrait: a small charcoal sketch of me in three-quarter profile. He delighted in the toilet set and the paperweight, but reserved his greatest praise for my poor sketch which he deemed "a perfect likeness."

In return he gave me a ruby promise ring inscribed with the phrase, "Love you, tomorrow" which I shall wear on my right hand until we can marry properly. He also gave me a small gold locket containing a lock of his raven hair and a collection of Byron's love poems.

He knows my heart, Marianne.

1838

Paris, France

January 5

Karl has written. He thanks me for sending Christmas gifts for the children and tells me that all is well in Weinheim. He mentions nothing about the end of our marriage. I realize I must once again write to him concerning that end and the agreement to begin our divorce proceedings this March. Too long have I danced with the truth.

January 7

I have hardened my heart, Marianne. The following letter is the result:

My husband,

I address you so, since you are my husband still, though I love another. Do you hope to change that fact by your persistent delays? If so, I can assure you that the love I bear for Spiros, and he for me will too persist, even if we must abandon our hopes for lawful marriage. And if our love, by some cruel act of fate, does not survive, I shall *still* not return to you.

I beg you, let me marry the man I have chosen. If you love me, let me fly.

Your Jeane

February 10

Today I received Karl's long-awaited, though difficult to read, reply:

My Jeanne,

I have asked my lawyer to proceed with our divorce. I shall not risk our friendship any longer with my attempts to delay.

I shall let you fly, though with your flight you abandon a loving husband and children for a man I believe to be of questionable character. Nevertheless, I shall strive to make the proceedings as private as possible to protect your future and the future of our children. I have asked my lawyer to contact your agent in Paris for the necessary negotiations.

Your husband,
Karl

March 2

With the coming of spring and the arrival of Karl's letter, Spiros and I can finally make plans for the future. I have begun learning Greek, though despite my facility with languages, I find the learning difficult. Greek possesses not only different letters from Germanic or Romance languages, but also different intonations and grammar. Luckily for me, my count is a patient teacher.

We also plan to visit London this summer for the coronation of Queen Victoria. I thought it the perfect opportunity to introduce Spiros to my family. Mama and Steely have agreed to meet him, though Papa will be away at sea. I am nervous at the prospect, though I hope that they will be as smitten with him as I am, Marianne.

London, England
June 20

Spiros and I arrived in London from Calais after a rough channel crossing to Dover, not to mention a harrowing coach ride to London and our destination, *Mivart's Hotel*. I have never seen the city more bustling - no doubt aided by the new railway lines that link the city to the surrounding countryside. It would seem that the whole of England has descended upon it to witness the coronation of Queen Victoria in eight day's time.

Tomorrow, Spiros and I will pay a call to 78 Harley Street for afternoon tea.

June 22

Yesterday Spiros and I ran the gauntlet. You think I exaggerate, my dear? By now you should know the character of La Madre, and the equally formidable Steely.

Our meeting began with exchanged pleasantries. Mama thanked Spiros for the gift of white roses, he thoughtfully had sent earlier in the day, while Steely remarked on the unusually hot weather. I agreed that the temperature was too warm for London which prompted Mama to ask Spiros whether this was his first visit to the city - to which he replied, "Yes, indeed." Mama then asked him, "And how do you find it?" He answered with a sly smile, "Not as hot as my homeland." We all laughed at his small joke and sat down.

After Mama served tea to each of us in turn, and we helped ourselves to egg and mayonnaise finger sandwiches, our conversation took a more direct and dangerous path. "My daughter tells me you wish to marry?" I tried to intervene, but Mama would have none of it. "I am speaking to your young man, Jane." Spiros quickly set down his tea cup to respond. Looking directly into her eyes, he said,

"You do not know me, my lady. For that reason you doubt my intentions, but I assure that I love your daughter and would willingly die for her. In fact, as you well know, I nearly did so. We will marry with or without your approval, but we would both much prefer with than without."

La Madre hesitated for a moment then replied, "Well said, young man." She then turned to me to ask whether we all might meet for the coronation.

Later I asked Spiros how he managed to find the right words to impress Mama. "I rehearsed them all week, my sweet," he answered with a wink.

My brave and darling man.

June 28

I am writing this after a long day, Marianne. It is not every day one witnesses history, so I thought to write down my observations before sleep steals the sounds and images from my mind:

The weather is fine with blue skies and a light wind which quickly lifts the morning fog to reveal the crowds lining the streets of the procession route, as Mama, Steely, Spiros, and I make our way through London by our carriage. Soon the queen's own carriage will carry her from her new home in Buckingham Palace to Westminster Abbey where the ceremony will take place before the peers of England and their guests.

The sounds of church bell, gun salute, and military band mix to charge the air with their cacophony as we reach our destination, the Gothic Cathedral that has witnessed the coronation of every British monarch since 1066. Once inside we sit in one of the special seating galleries created especially for today. Mama sniffs a bit at our seating - she is now, after all, the daughter of an earl - but I enjoy the vantage point offered by our balcony perch. I can look down upon princes, princesses, dukes, duchesses, as well as foreign dignitaries without being noticed in return. I see former friends from Almack's: Countess Lieven and Count Apponyi. Suddenly apprehensive about my past, I nervously ask Steely whether she has seen Lord Ellenborough. She replies no, but adds unhelpfully, "Meeting up with him today could prove awkward."

Presently a hush comes over the crowd, as the orchestra of some eighty musicians and twice as many singers begin performing, "I Was Glad," upon the entrance of Her Majesty, soon followed by "God Save Our Queen." She, looking far too young for a queen, wears a gown of white lace with red velvet and gold brocade trimmed with ermine. After the especially long Litany and Sermon, a blessedly short Prayer is said. However, amid the pomp and circumstance a human touch occurs, elderly Lord Rolle stumbles to the floor before the queen who assists him to his feet unharmed. Decorum restored, she is then crowned by the Archbishop of Canterbury with a crown laden with jewels including the Black Prince's Ruby and the Stuart Sapphire. Trumpets sound; Handel is played. The Benediction and Homage are given; Communion is taken and *Hallelujah* is sung. God is indeed praised, the five hour long service has ended.

As we stifle yawns and slowly make our way out of Westminster, silver Coronation medals are thrown to the crowd. Spiros manages to catch one which he gives to me, saying, "For *my* Queen."

My gallant.

Paris, France

July 11

We have returned to France and to our perpetual state of waiting. Karl *did* warn me that our divorce might take months, even years, to finalize; however, I fear that Karl procrastinates *again*. Regardless, we bide our time in the pursuit of linguistics. I continue learning Greek, gaining some proficiency. And I have taken to improving his French. Each time after we make love he tells me, "Peut-être sommes nous pere et mere maintenant." I have never wanted a man's child more, Marianne.

August 10

I believe I am at long last with child, though I shall wait one more month to tell Spiros. For now it will be my secret.

September 15

On his twenty-sixth birthday I revealed that secret to Spiros. I waited until after dining at the *Le Grand Vefour* with the *Tout-Paris* - pretending we could afford such extravagances every day of the week. As we walked home in the full moon of the mild late summer, I asked - rather nonchalantly I think - whether he would like a boy or a girl. He stopped immediately and turned to me to ask, "You are. . . *enceinte*? I nodded in response and asked again, "A boy or girl?" He thought for a moment and said, "A girl, I think - then she will be able to spoil her little brother."

Bright moonlight followed us home.

September 20

I have spent today writing letters. To Mama and Papa. To Kenelm. To Aunt Anne and, of course, to Karl. To my family I wrote freely, telling them of my pregnancy, as well as our hopes for marriage and eagerness to begin anew. To my husband I wrote more guardedly, telling *him* of my pregnancy and that he must now *more than ever* accept our marriage as dissolved and to proceed with dispatch at making that truth official. I also asked whether he wished for me to return the gimmel ring and the heirloom jewel-case he had given me during our marriage.

I shall see if my words take root.

October 1

Karl has written. I have included his response below:

My dear wife,

I have urged my lawyer to prepare the papers for our divorce directly, given the news of your latest letter. I have rebelled for the last time against the harshness of my destiny. If I have wronged you, I swear that my intentions were always good. I have never loved anyone as I have loved you.

Do not think to return the ring or the jewel-case. I will never have another woman to whom I would wish to give them. I will have female friends, perhaps a mistress, but I will never have another Jeane.

I wish you only good fortune.

Yours,
Karl

I do not know which is greater, my guilt or my relief.

November 10

 My love has gone once again to Greece and once again I am alone, though not. The child is ever present. I have taken to calling her - or him - *to moro mas*, Greek for *our baby*, since its quickening. I have even taken to talking and singing to the little mite as it moves within me, though our conversation is a trifle one-sided. Nevertheless, Eugenie assures me that a child in the womb loves to hear the sound of its mother's voice. Can *to moro mas* really hear me? Since it is such a pleasant thought, I shall choose to believe it.

December 2

Spiros has returned to us this Advent with wonderful news. His parents have given their blessings to our plans to marry, despite their earlier misgivings. They however insist that we marry in the Greek Orthodox

Church which would require my conversion, which would in turn requires a period of six months instruction in the faith.

I agree without hesitation. Perhaps I shall find belief again.

1839

I have disappeared into my own happiness. When a fear or misgiving surfaces they vanish in a blink of an eye. I am impervious to the doubt that has plagued my past.

My only complaint is a lack of physical intimacy, a lack which I blame upon the Parisian accoucheur employed by Spiros. Monsieur Gaudet prescribes no relations during pregnancy among other uncompromising restrictions. How I do wish for the common sense midwifery of Sophia! Male midwives think nothing of ordering their patients about, making the most natural of processes a scientific endeavour.

Nevertheless, Spiros and I do find ways to adjust to the prescribed restrictions. He first showers my face, neck, breasts, and belly with kisses. I protest, citing doctor's orders. He then moves even lower saying, "There are other ways to give pleasure."

Indeed there are, Marianne.

February 1

My divorce from Karl has been granted, though under German law the conditions are severe. I may never again set foot in Bavaria or Wurttemberg. However, now Spiros and I can finally plan for our future. After the birth of our child in March, we hope to marry as soon as possible in a simple Greek Orthodox ceremony here in Paris. We will then prepare for our move to Greece on the island of Tinos, where his father is now governor. Our future awaits us there.

March 10

Our son was born yesterday after a birth so sudden and swift that Monsieur Gaudet arrived too late for his duties. My resourceful Eugenie, aided by a reluctant

Spiros, delivered him safely in less than two hours. Later as I lay with him in my arms with his father by my side, we decided upon his name, *Leonidas*, meaning the son of the lion, after the great warrior king of Sparta.

March 17

My count has gone to London to tell my family about the birth of Leonidas and to seek my father's approval of my hand in marriage. I assured him that no such gesture was needed, but Spiros insisted that he see my father before Papa leaves for his naval duties at the end of the month.

I find myself spending much of my time in the nursery with our son, something I never did with any of my other children. His nurses tell me he sleeps and feeds well and rarely cries - such a good boy. I can while away afternoons rocking him in his cradle, playing my lute softly, and reading the final installment of *Oliver Twist*.

Sweet Oliver has found his family just as I have found mine.

April 10

We are married at long last.

With Papa's approval granted, though regrettably without his presence, Spiros and I were wed in a small Greek Orthodox ceremony here in Paris with Mama, Steely, Kenelm and a handful of Spiros's fellow compatriots from Marseilles looking on.

In accordance with Greek custom, Spiros and I stand before a small table in which two candles, two crowns called *stefana*, a Bible, and a cup of wine are placed. We say no vows. Instead we exchange rings which are blessed by the priest. We then hold lighted candles representing the sacrament. To seal our union we are crowned as the king and queen of our life together. Three times the crowns are exchanged by the *koumbaro*, the witness to our joining. The priest then reads from the Epistle of St. Paul who advises us to, "Be subject to one another under reverence to Christ" as we hold right hands. We drink the ceremonial wine and then the priest proclaims us husband and wife before he removes our crowns. Finally, we take our first steps as a married couple with the priest's blessing to go in peace.

I shall pray to God that his blessing will follow us to Tinos, my new home.

1843

My dear friend, I have just come across you - hiding behind dust and cobwebs in my wardrobe - neglected in the making of my new home but not forgotten. I thought of you often, and would say to myself at such times, "I really must tell Marianne about this . . . or that." Yet I did not. Life intervened, happily so.

Now, I must recall for you almost four years - but where shall I begin? Perhaps it is best to start with my island home in the Cyclades archipelago:

I still remember my first sight of Tinos. After having travelled over one thousand miles, Spiros, Leonidas, and I - with, of course, the inestimable Eugenie - had finally come to the last leg of our journey. From a port in Athens, Greece we took a ferry to the most beautiful island in the Aegean sea. Surrounded by a sea bluer than the azure sky, the white sands and white-washed buildings of Tinos reflected a brilliant sun as we disembarked. A country road through steep, rocky slopes brought us to a modest house overlooking the ocean. Spiros worried that it might not meet my expectations.

"Nonsense," I recall saying. My mind had already begun to place the rugs and furniture that I had sent ahead on its stone floors. I imagined my sketches and watercolors, both past and future, filling its plaster walls. Feather tick pillows and cotton quilts covered the master bed. Leonidas's antique cradle stood by the nursery window so that he could smell the salt air as a sea breeze caressed him. In our new home.

March 20

Not long after we arrived in Tinos, the governor, Spiros's father, gave a reception in our honor with prominent townspeople, as well as the Theotoky clan in attendance. If my reputation preceded me, my husband's family gave no hint of it in our first meeting. Their warmth and acceptance was a balm to my spirit. I remember Spiro's mother, Angelica, a lovely woman with liquid brown eyes, asking me how I would fill my days without the pleasures of Paris or London to occupy me. I believe I answered, "The pleasures of Paris and London are overestimated. I look forward to simpler ones here."

And I do find simple pleasures . . . our island is small, but it holds many secrets which Spiros and I discover. We explore slopes so stony that no horse could hold its footing there. On such hikes we come across ruins of the past, the most remarkable being *Kionia*, the temple of Poseidon, half buried underneath the dirt of a millennium. When Leonidas grows old enough we take him with us to the island's many beaches where he plays in the white sand wearing only his napkin - or he squeals with delight when his father and mother dip him in the warm water of the Aegean.

Some days we pursue more decorous activities such as attending dinner parties hosted by my husband's parents at the governor's house or visiting Our Lady of Tinos, a shrine whose icon supposedly foretold the success of the Greek revolution and performs such miracles that Greeks conduct pilgrimages to it each year on the fifteenth of August.

Here on Tinos I have found freedom and love - *phila* born of *eros*. From passion comes amity.

April 4

For my thirty-fourth birthday Spiros planned an excursion to the neighboring island of Delos. For the day, we acted as tourists, travelling on the steam-powered ferry that services the numerous islands in the Aegean. With other curiosity seekers we arrived at the island known as the birthplace of Apollo. Many of these seekers expressed disappointment with the barren landscape of Delos, but I found its ruins fascinating, as Spiros knew I would. Something about ancient civilizations has always captured my imagination. Here I could imagine, among the jumble of stones tangled beneath vine and scrub, the island's Colossus and Theatre brought back to their former glory. Surely archaeologists of the future must explore the island's ruins and excavate them, just like the ruins of Pompeii have been.

If only I could be part of such an endeavor, Marianne.

April 20

La Madre and Aunt Anne would disapprove of the way I
dote upon my son. British women of privilege do not
raise their children, the servants do. This model of
femininity was one I followed, until Leonidas. The
change in my behavior I attribute partly to the
boundless love of children seen here in Greece and
partly to the beguiling mix of his mother and father that
I see in our son. He looks like me, the same fair skin,
blue eyes, and fine hair just one shade darker than
mine, but he has, even at age four, the movement and
gestures of his father. He strides with feet splayed
outward in a dancer's stride like his *pateras*. They both
raise one eyebrow when asking a question. My son
though also possesses qualities *both* his parents share.
He is daring. He climbs anything, be it tree, fence, or
rocky slope. He loves animals, especially his gentle
tabby who lets him place his head on her tummy -
asking me just yesterday with one brow arched, "Have
you ever heard the insides of a cat, Mama?" To which I
replied, "Not lately."

I regret that I cannot give him a sister or brother, though Spiros and I are determined to try, again and again.

May 11

Letters from England and Germany have arrived. Steely writes with both satisfying and troubling news. Papa has been made a full Admiral of the Blue, after his many years of service in the Royal Navy. However he took a bad fall from which he has been slow to recover, even with Mama's faithful care. Steely tells me not to worry, but of course I do. I wish I could run to him despite the thousand miles that separate us. A daughter has only one father.

Steely also sends two collections of Hans Christian Andersen tales, since I had complained in my last letter about my difficulty finding books here in Greece written in English. I intend to read the stories with Leo to help him learn his mother's tongue. He is after all half British. I shall send my latest sketch of him in thanks for her thoughtfulness.

Karl also writes. He tells me the children are well and that he thinks of me often. I regret that I do not think of him, or them, often enough.

June 2

Spiros's father has asked him to manage his family's estate in Doukades, Corfu. Our move there is planned for early August. I am torn between sadness at leaving our island home and excitement at starting anew. Spiros of course welcomes the opportunity to return to his childhood home.

July 10

Kenelm writes with sad news. My grandfather has died at eighty-eight years old. His death was sudden. He fell ill on June 29th and passed only one day later. His last words were fitting enough, "Well, perhaps I have talked too much." Despite our estrangement, I still remember the great man fondly.

Mama, according to my brother, received the news as well as can be expected, but has been comforted by dear Papa's improvement in the past few days, an improvement in which I too find solace.

Long live King Coke of Holkham Hall.

I never thought that I missed the color green until our arrival on Corfu. Unlike Tinos and many other Greek isles that appear to be scrubbed clean of soil and plant, Corfu bursts with shades of green that rival those of an English countryside. In fact, Britain and Corfu share surprising similarities. In addition to both being islands, they also possess lowlands and smaller isles, as well as mountains nearly three thousand feet high. They also share diplomatic ties. As a protectorate of Britain since 1815, the island has prospered with improved roads and water systems, even the building of a university, the first in Greece. Yet it remains quintessentially Grecian with its remains of antiquity and the warmth of its climate, its people.

The Theotoky family estate lies just outside of Doukades, a village with rolling hills perfect for its many orchards and vineyards. Today as we ride through the acres of olive and grape, my husband tells Leo and me about how he and his older brother, Nicolo, would roam those rolling hills, catching tortoises or scaring hedgehogs. "I followed him everywhere as a child," he said. "Even as an adult, I follow him here in managing Papa's estate." Soon we arrive at a sprawling mansion made of soft grey and brown stone with a terracotta tile roof. The burning August sun is soon forgotten in its cool rooms where servants treat our son to mint lemonade and his parents to *mastika* over ice in honor of our arrival. The traditional liqueur turns white over the ice and tastes of cedar.

We are home again.

August 19

Knowing how much I missed riding, Spiros has surprised me with a new horse, a white Arabian who I call Athos, in honor of my favorite Musketeer. Has it really been over five years since I have been astride?

First pregnancy, then the rocky ground of Tinos - quite unsuitable for horses - are to blame.

This morning I rose early to ride miles down a serpentine path to the seaside, enjoying the cool air and the sole companionship of Athos. My lovely boy has a soft mouth and responds to the slightest movement of my leg or hand.

August 20

I had forgotten about the unique pain of saddle sore, Marianne.

August 26

Recovered, I rode yesterday with my husband by the path I discovered to a small isolated beach. Although he is a reasonably good horseman, the hilly terrain challenges his skill. Truly I possess a far better seat, though of course I keep that knowledge to myself.

We stopped for a picnic lunch - a bottle of his family's label and folded unleavened bread filled with veal, tomatoes, and tangy *yoghurd* sauce - partaken on a faded quilt on soft warm sand. Later with only gulls to see us I seduced my husband. We made love accompanied by their cries and the crescendo of the rising tide.

September 2

My darling Babou has passed away. I received word from Mama in a letter dated July 20th, one day after his death, a death most likely caused, according to his doctor, by complications from his fall earlier in the year. Just think, Marianne, when I was enjoying the making of my new home, happy in my love for my husband and child, my father lay dying. I cannot help thinking that I should have been there beside him. I should have travelled the many miles to see him one last time and comfort him as I could. Yet I did not.

He was seventy-two. Odd that I was surprised by the sum of years that he lived. He always seemed ageless to me. I remember how his face never failed to light up when he saw me. How he taught me to ride, not trusting the grooms at Forston to take proper care with me. How he always kissed the top of my head before leaving to sail the seas. I was his first child.

Mama, with her unerring ability to say the wrong thing, warned in her letter that death comes in threes. I really should not blame her though, she has lost both father and husband in the span of months. I will try to keep that thought close when I write her.

1844

Doukades
Corfu, Greece
March 2

I received a letter today from the lawyer handling the wills of my late father and grandfather. It would seem that their bequests have made me a wealthy woman. I shall make arrangements that a portion of that wealth be set aside for my children, Matilde, Herberto, Berthe, and of course, Leonidas, who remains my surest comfort in my grief.

After nearly eight months since his death, I still find myself mourning the loss of my father. I cannot shake the feeling that I could have done more for him. I wrote as much to Mama, who wrote back, admonishing me for such a thought. She asked, rightly so, "What *could* have you done?" But still . . .

I find that I cannot sleep through the night. The first time I slipped from our bed with my restlessness Spiros said the following morning, "I reached for you, but you weren't there." Now he greets me each morning with a coolness that frightens me. But still, I cannot sleep.

Bagni a Corsena, Italy
April 1

I assure you that no land is more beautiful than Tuscany in April. We are here at Spiro's insistence that I should take the waters to cure my lingering despondency. I am glad that he did. Though I cannot speak for the waters as yet, our travels to get here have already lightened my spirits. My husband, son, and I sailed the Adriatic upon a sloop and rode by carriage through chestnut forests reported to be patrolled by brigands. Alas, to Leo's disappointment, we met none, arriving safely at our destination, a rented villa, with fortunes intact.

The village of *Bagni a Corsena* is located in the Lima valley surrounded on all sides by mountains. Two natural steam caves, *Grotto Grande* and *Grotto Paolina*, once used by Etruscans and Romans have been more recently used by such famous personages as Dante, Dumas, Napoleon, Shelley, and Byron. Today British and French tourists visit the caves to cure what ails them. Tomorrow we shall see them for ourselves.

April 2

Spiro and I take the waters.

Grotto Paolino, named after Napoleon' sister no less, is
the smaller of the two grottoes and accommodates
women. Grotto Grande is reserved for men. Once again,
society's separation of the sexes inhibits enjoyment,
but the experience is well worth the ghastly smell - to
which one *does* become accustomed - and the less than
ideal company.

Wearing only a linen chemise, I slip into steaming
waters at first too hot, then straight away just warm
enough to melt muscle and sinew. Ignoring the chatter
of the women about me. I lay languorous and liquid
until I can lay no longer.

Later, upon returning to our villa after our evening dip,
I immediately fall into bed and sleep as I have not slept
in months.

April 3

Today I am thirty-six. I wake to the soft kisses of my husband who like me, smells vaguely of sulfur. We choose to ignore our mutual malodor as we join in the soft light of dawn. Soon spent, we fall asleep again until the late morning sun wakes us.

Later we rise and bathe, ordering breakfast in room and linger over *cornetto* and milky coffee until our son joins us, impatient with our tardiness. "I wanted to say, 'Happy Birthday,' to you earlier, Mama, but Nurse wouldn't let me," he pouts. We spend the perfect spring day walking the village and surrounding countryside, allowing our son to lead the way.

After dinner Spiros and I try our hands at the casino created for the tourists of Bagni a Corsena. As my lack of luck (and skill) would have it, I lose miserably at baccarat. My husband however wins at the roulette wheel with an inside bet on red thirty-six, in honor of my birthday.

"My winnings almost cover its cost," he says later at our villa as he hands me a box wrapped with red velvet ribbon. Inside is a pear-shaped opal solitaire pendant with gold chain. I marvel at the stone's play of color with its flash of yellow, orange, green, blue, and purple. "I understand it comes from Russia," he tells me.

I model the necklace for him later, wearing nothing else.

Doukades
Corfu, Greece
May 1

We are to move once again, Marianne. Spiros has received an appointment to the King of Greece's court as his personal secretary. King Otto, who you may or may not remember, is the son of King Ludwig of Bavaria. King Otto of Greece is young and deeply unpopular in his adopted country.

Life has just become more complicated.

Athens, Greece

June 10

Athens. Ancient city of Greece. Cradle of Western Civilization. Birthplace of Democracy. Now, little more than a poor village still suffering from the aftermath of the Greek revolution. Nearly ten years battling the oppression of Turkish rule, another ten under the rule of a Bavarian king, the people of Greece now at long last have been granted a constitution and Greek citizens, such as my husband, have some small measure of power in their country. Here is where we begin again.

Despite his unpopularity, I found the young king charming, though lacking the energy and strength of character of his father, when I was introduced to him during a diplomatic garden party shortly after our arrival in Athens. Kissing my hand in welcome, Otto - as he insisted I call him - told me that his father still speaks of me, his *Ianthe*, fondly. Without thinking I insisted, since we were on a first name basis, that he too call me Ianthe. I then turned to greet the king's wife, Amalia, who gave me such a withering look that I realized immediately that I had just made a dreadful mistake. My reputation has surely preceded me. Again.

Later I told my husband about my *faux pas* before the queen. He laughed in response, saying that only the king's opinion of me mattered.

Of that, I am not sure.

June 20

While Spiros attends to his duties to the king, I spend my days in consultation with the architect, Stamatios Kleanthes, who is to design our new home on land I purchased near the king's palace. How many times have I created a new home? My best recollection is eight times. I never tire of it, frankly.

My latest undertaking has been inspired by the Palladian style of Holkham Hall though smaller in scale - a style in keeping with the new Athens. Kleanthes, who also designed the city's British embassy, promises he will have the house built before winter, a tall order. We shall see.

One would think that living in a hotel would appeal to my bohemian spirit. However, I have learned that my wanderlust needs tempering by my need for belonging. Our hotel offers only temporary accommodation and fleeting acquaintances. British, French Italian, and German tourists stay a week or two to glimpse the ancient world then disappear only to be replaced by more of the same. Here, in *Hotel Europe* as we call it, the only permanent residents besides Spiros, Leonidas, and I are another married couple with a young son, Konstantinos and Ecaterina Dosios, who like us await the building of their new home. This similitude has made us fast friends. We dine together, our sons play together, and we see, like the tourists, the ancient ruins together.

Yesterday we toured the Acropolis which, because of its rocky hillside perch, is visible throughout the city. Within its complex, the Acropolis contains many temples and theatres of antiquity, though few rival the Parthenon. Though damaged by age and military conflict, the Parthenon still evokes its former majesty. Its immense Doric columns rise to the heavens and loom over poor mortals such as we who stand below, trying to imagine what the temple looked like in the age of Pericles. We had been told that once a gold and ivory statue of the goddess Athena stood within. She stood forty feet tall and held Nike, the goddess of Victory, in her right hand. Now nothing of her remains.

Later we saw the Theatre of Dionysus where excavations are still underway. Here drama was born. Here the plays of Sophocles, Euripides, Aeschylus, and Aristophanes were performed. Here, during the fifth century, actors played Oedipus, Antigone, Medea, or Prometheus to as many as seventeen thousand people.

Today however a different scene plays upon its stage. Four friends escape the heat of a summer day under the shade of a cypress tree, sharing a picnic lunch and a bottle of *Athiri* white wine. Two small boys, one fair, the other dark, play pretend amongst the rubble of the once great amphitheater. Leonidas and Aristeidis fight atop the *theatron*, the stone seating area that stretches up a stony slope, using sticks as swords. To our horror we watch as Leonidas slips and tumbles down some twenty feet. Spiros and I run to him who, to our relief, we find only stunned - a bloody knee and a skinned elbow his only injuries. "I'm not hurt, Mama," he says as I gather him into my arms.

Just another scrape in the life of Leonidas Theotoky.

September 10

With cooling temperatures the royal court of King Otto
begins its social season. Last night I danced for the first
time with my husband. Odd that that is the case, but
our tumultuous courtship and the quiet isolation of the
early years in our marriage did not lend itself to social
niceties. Unfortunately, I learned that Spiros's innate
physical grace cannot make up for his lack of
experience upon the ballroom floor. Thrice he asked
me to pardon his clumsy footwork during our waltz. On
the other hand, King Otto's dancing skills are
admirable, no doubt honed by his years at his father's
court. When we danced the mazurka he complimented
me on my own skill, as well as my beautiful eyes,
though his own returned repeatedly to my decolletage.
My response was cool, knowing that his wife observed
us. One withering glance from her is more than enough,
thank you. Besides, I am still *very* much in love with my
own husband.

October 4

At great expense, I have had my horse, Athos, sent the three hundred miles from Corfu to me here in Athens. Now I can enjoy the pleasures of his company, since the pleasure of my husband's is often in short supply with the demands of his obligations to the king. In addition to riding in the outskirts of the city, I have taken to riding in the Royal Garden, one of the many improvements made by Otto in his efforts to rebuild Athens. The park is said by some to have been built over the remains of the *Lyceum*, where Aristotle and Socrates once taught. Now however the park is home to Judas and eucalyptus trees, as well as oleanders.

As I ride enjoying this green heart of Athens, I happen upon, to my surprise, the king who is also enjoying a ride on this cool autumn day. He asks to accompany me and, without waiting for an answer, begins to tell me about the conservatory in the park where new specimens of exotic plants are cultivated by his "clever wife." I think how much he is like his father in his love of improvement projects and in his appreciation of women - although I must admit his attentions to *me* make me uneasy. Is it only my vanity or does he wish to be like his father in his choice of a mistress?

November 3

Stamatios, our architect, has kept his word. Our new home will be completed in time for the holidays. For now, I spend my days, with dear Eugenie's assistance, ordering furnishings, draperies, and deciding upon the most fetching floral wallpaper designs. We are also interviewing locals to fill positions for housekeeping, kitchen, and garden duties. The Count and I have also decided to hire a tutor for our son who has outgrown his nurses in his headlong pursuit of boyhood. Luckily, we found the perfect young man, a Mr. Woodcock, an Englishman who speaks perfect Greek and is a recent graduate of the University of Athens. His imposing stature though gentle demeanor have even impressed Leonidas who had asked (or should I say, demanded?) that he approve of our choice for his tutor.

December 21

Tonight we will host our first party, a housewarming for the new residence of the Count and Countess Theotoky. After living in a hotel for over seven months, we look forward with great pleasure to entertaining friends in our new home. We expect twenty-two guests, a mix of British and Greek diplomats, most of whom are as young as we. I requested on the invitations that anyone who accepts must promise *not* to discuss politics. As you well know Marianne, politics and pleasure do not mix, especially at Yuletide!

December 22

It has taken most of the day for the staff to clear the wreckage produced by high spirits and too much *ouzo*. It goes without saying that our housewarming was a great success. We tittle-tattled and chin-wagged. We tucked into and quaffed. We circle-danced, clasping hands as we moved right then left and back, back, and back again. Later the dancing progressed - or perhaps descended - into a decidedly masculine competition. Our great friend, Konstantinos, challenged Spiros to the *Zeibekiko*, an improvised folk dance to be performed upon a marble tabletop which cracked under their efforts. In an attempt to prevent further damage to our home, I immediately declared Konstantinos the winner.

My husband and I decided to keep the table to serve as a reminder of a most memorable night. May we have many more.

December 24

After the raucous celebration of a few days ago, Spiros and I are happy to enjoy the remainder of Yuletide quietly in our home. Today we decorated both Christmas tree and Christmas boat, a combination of German and Greek traditions made popular by King Otto. After we finished our trimming Leonidas asked if we might launch the Christmas boat upon one of the small lakes in the nearby Royal Gardens. We agreed, sending the small craft adrift to the delight of our son.

Later, the three of us shared Christmas bread flavored with cinnamon, cloves, and orange topped with a doughy cross. Our indulgence was interrupted by the sound of voice and percussion outside. We opened the front door to find a group of boys singing *kalanda*, or carols, in the streets, accompanied by drums and triangles. As a reward for their efforts, Spiros tossed them small silver coins called *lepta*. Leonidas of course wished to join them, but I convinced him that if he did so *Ayios Vassileios* would not know where to deliver his gifts. Tomorrow after all is Christmas day.

1845

The new year begins with marvelous news from
Kenelm. My brother is now the father of a healthy
daughter. His wife, Emily, is doing well. Mama delights
in her newest granddaughter who is called Jane
Elizabeth after both grandmother and aunt. I shall send
our namesake a gold locket that I purchased last year in
Italy.

Kenelm also informs me that London society has taken
to calling me "the female Byron" in "honor of my
romantic escapes." It would seem that one member of
my family has finally accepted or, at the very least, is
amused by my notoriety, Marianne!

February 6

I invited my dear friend, Ecatrina, to tea. During her
call, our conversation turned, as our conversations will,
to *bavardage* concerning the king and queen. She
teased me about Otto's attentions to me and that,
rumor has it, his queen is jealous of that attention.
Ecatrina has heard, from a reliable source of course,
that she also refuses to hear any talk about "that
Countess Theotoky" especially anything that shows me
in a favorable light. I laughed and said it was simply
idle talk. In response Ecatrina reminded me, no longer
teasing, that there is nothing *idle* about the displeasure
of a queen.

March 9

Leonidas's sixth birthday. Today he was spoiled as any
child can be by his grandparents. From England our son
received a kaleidoscope and hoop and stick. From
Tinos, a *Tavli* set, a game similar to backgammon, and a
bag of lemon drops. His doting parents gave him a
Kokoni, a small silky-haired and curly-tailed pup with a

sweet disposition who our son promptly named Turk, after the dog in *The Swiss Family Robinson*, his latest favorite book.

We spent the day at a beach with shallow waters near *Vouliagmeni*, playing in the sun so long that my husband grew as swarthy as a pirate, while his fair-skinned wife and child burned red. As we walked to our carriage for the ride home, Leonidas said, "We should do that more often, Papa."

I agree.

March 25

Today is Greek Independence Day, the day the entire country celebrates its freedom from Ottoman rule. Spiros is again busy with his duties for the king. Nevertheless, Leonidas, Eugenie, Mr. Woodcock and I will enjoy the day walking the city without him. As my son runs ahead playing hoop and stick, his tutor relishes his role as historian. He recalls for us the revolts against the Turks that occurred throughout Greece from 1821 until 1832. He tells of the long battle for freedom so passionately that Eugenie remarks that he should seek employment as tour guide to Athens.

"Perhaps I shall, Mademoiselle," the young man responds with a blush.

With Mr. Woodcock's words to remind us of that war, the continued Ottoman presence in the city strikes me as curious. Athens is as *kosmos politikos* as any great European city with international visitors of all sorts, but to see Turkish Muslims mingle peacefully with Greek Christians on this day especially illustrates to me one of the pleasant ironies of war. Mortal enemies may be transformed into friends.

April 3

I have lived thirty-seven years, a number that surprises me. My youthfulness thankfully continues. I suppose it is my luck to have inherited the Coke family's stubborn resistance to the aging process.

As I write these words, Spiros approaches me from behind and whispers, "Happy Birthday," cupping my breasts with his hands. His lips on the nape of my neck raise gooseflesh. Pardon me, Marianne - it would seem my husband demands my immediate attention.

May 10

Just when I had given up all hope, I find myself again with child. Although Eugenie told me I should wait to tell Spiros, I could not. Both happy and surprised by my pregnancy, he insists I see a doctor.

May 14

I find my doctor a disagreeable man, Marianne. After a cursory examination Dr. Anastas confirmed that I was indeed pregnant and added, "I suggest no riding or marital relations - especially at your age."

Especially at my age?

June 6

Despite my heeding the suggestions of Dr. Anastas, I have lost our child. The doctor tells us that more children are unlikely.

September 1

My physical recuperation has been quick, though my spirit is slow to recover. I suggest a trip abroad to Spiros, but he is far too busy with the demands of the king. He promises that we will go to Italy after the holidays.

To fill the hours I read. At Mr. Woodcock's suggestion I borrow his copy of Miss Elizabeth Barrett's *Poems*, a collection which has gained much critical acclaim in England. My favorite poem is "A Lady's Yes."

"Yes!" I answered you last night.
"No," this morning, Sir, I say!
Colours, seen by candle-light,
Will not look the same by day.

When the tabors play the best,
Lamps above, laughs below -
Love me sounded like a jest,
Fit for *Yes*, or fit for *No*!

Call me false, or call me free -

Vow, whatever light might shine,
No man on your face shall see
Any grief for change on mine.

Yet the sin is on us both -
Time to dance is not to woo -
Wooer light makes fickle troth -
Scorn of *me* recoils on *you*.

Learn to win a lady's faith
Nobly as the thing is high.
Bravely, as for life or death -
With a loyal gravity.

Lead her from the festive boards,
Point her to the starry skies,
Guard her, by your truthful words,
Pure from courtship's flatteries.

By your truth, she shall be true -
Be ever true as wives of yore -
And her *Yes*, once said to you,
SHALL be Yes for evermore.

October 19

Tonight Spiros and I attended a gala at court, the first since our loss. I noticed my husband dancing with a young woman I did not recognize. He held her far too closely and looked at her with a look I know too well.

November 30

I recall Lord Ellenborough's behavior. The inordinate amount of time spent away from home. The evasive answers to any questions. I see the same behavior now.

December 20

My suspicions are confirmed. I found a note in his jacket with words difficult to misinterpret:

Darling -
Think of last night when you read these words.
C.

I showed Eugenie the note. She told me that she too had her suspicions, but did not wish to tell me of them without proof.

Do I seek that proof or not, Marianne?

December 22

"You cannot let such a small thing stand between us?" he said to me after I confronted him with my suspicions. "You too have had your *flirtations*."

"Are you suggesting that I sleep with King Otto?

"It is you who has suggested it, my dear."

It was as though I spoke with a stranger - such small things indeed.

December 26

This yuletide my husband and I played the happy family for our son's sake, though our marriage grows cold.

Today I told him that I will leave with Eugenie and Leonidas for Italy next week. I expected some argument but instead he replied, "Perhaps we *should* part for a while."

December 31

Tomorrow I leave with Eugenie and Leonidas for Bagni a Corsena. Leonidas asked why Papa is not coming along with us. I tell him that Papa has other affairs to which he must attend.

I grow cynical.

1846

I arrived at our villa late last night with Eugenie and Leonidas in tow. Throughout our journey here I brooded over my husband's betrayal. I ask myself the same questions over and over:

Do I forgive him or not? If I do forgive, can I ever trust him again? Can I still love him? If I cannot, how can I remain in a marriage bereft of trust or love? If I do not forgive him, how do I find the courage to begin anew at thirty-seven and with a six-year-old son? Could I find love again? Would I want to love again?

My brooding has yet to produce any answers.

- A simple child,

That lightly draws its breath,

And feels its life in every limb,

What should it know of death?

- William Wordsworth

January 15

A small body falls quickly, far more quickly than mind can grasp or muscle respond.

"Mama, look," I hear Leonidas say. I look up to see him balancing upon the handrail of the staircase balcony. One moment he loses his footing, the next he plummets to the marble floor. I run, hoping to catch him.

 I am too late.

January 18

Today I bury my son.

For three days I have coordinated the grim logistics of death. I arranged for a local woman to lay out his body, for the undertaker to take the measurements for his coffin. I wrote to my husband telling him of our son's death. I asked that he might come to me, though he cannot arrive in time for the service that I have arranged to be conducted by a visiting Greek Orthodox priest in a nearby Anglican church.

For three days I have neither slept nor ate. Though my rebel heart be broken, I cannot cry. You instead must cry for me, and for him, my Marianne.

To Be Continued

Volume Three of *Jane Digby's Diary, Following an Eastern Star*, is available in Amazon's Kindle Store.

A Note about Code

Jane frequently wrote in code in her diaries, perhaps in fear that someone might read her most private thoughts without her permission. I too include short passages in code whenever she reveals something of a truly private or incriminating nature. For the code I chose a Caesar D cipher - the key to which I have included on the next page for those readers who would like to be privy to Jane's most intimate declarations:

D=A
E=B
F=C
G=D
H=E
I=F
J=G
K=H
L=I
M=J
N=K
O=L
P=M
Q=N
R=O
S=P
T=Q
U=R
V=S
W=T
X=U
Y=V
Z=W
A=X
B=Y

C=Z

Author's Note

I suspect most writers of historical fiction have struggled with the distinction between historical fact and historical fiction. I too have struggled with how to best represent the historical Jane with the Jane of my imagination. Much is known about the real Jane, indeed three biographies have been written about her. Some of her correspondence has survived, as well as some of her diaries, though much was lost, or perhaps destroyed by a disapproving descendent it is thought. What else we know of Jane comes from the writings of her contemporaries, who knew her or knew of her. The rest must be filled between the lines, much like crayoning the spaces of a sketch in a coloring book.

I believe I have stayed true to Jane's character, despite my reconstructions of the realities of her life. I have changed dates and chronologies to better suit the demands of a diary format and combined or embellished characters where I thought necessary. I have even created incidents in her life when I thought some justification was needed for her actions. And although I have tried to avoid anachronisms, I also wanted Jane's voice to sound contemporary enough that my readers could imagine her as any young woman, not merely one from 19th century Britain. I am convinced her story is one that can bridge the span of more than a century.

I strived - and will continue to strive - to create the best Jane I can, to do justice to a remarkable woman who led an extraordinary life.

Acknowledgements

First and foremost, I would like to acknowledge three biographies written about Jane Digby that were crucial in my research of her life: *Odyssey of a Loving Woman* by E.M. Oddie, *Passion's Child* by Margaret Fox Schmidt, and *A Scandalous Life: The Biography of Jane Digby* by Mary S. Lovell. The first two biographies are no longer in print, though the Lovell biography is available in print and as an ebook. I highly recommend it for readers who would like to know more about Jane's scandalous life.

In addition, I also recommend *The Wilder Shores of Love* by Lesley Blanch. A compilation of stories about 19th century women who "followed the beckoning Eastern Star," the book includes a biography profile and commentary concerning what led Jane Digby to find her heart and home in Syria.

I would also like to thank the numerous writers whose websites I visited for research to help me bring to life the customs, locales, and personages of the early 19th century in a textured way. I consulted more than I can mention here, but I would like to acknowledge some of my favorites:

Kathryn Kane's *The Regency Redingote*
Vic Sanborn's *Jane Austen's World*
Shannon Selin, *Imaging the Bounds of History*

And, of course, the many anonymous and often unpaid writers and researchers at *Britannica.com*, *Encyclopedia.com*, and *Wikipedia*. Where would any fact-checking novelist be without them?

I would also like to acknowledge the online map of Europe after 1815 by Alexander Altenhof that I used for my own research and reference, so that I might describe Jane's journey across post-Napoleonic Europe with historical accuracy.

And last but not least, I thank my husband, Ken, who acts as my proofreader, editor, and sounding board. I love you more than you know.

And one more thing . . .

Independent authors like me need the support of readers like you. If you have enjoyed *Jane Digby's Diary*, please leave a review on Amazon and/or Goodreads.

Thank you,
CR

About the Author

C.R. Hurst, who taught writing and language at a small college in Pennsylvania for over 25 years, retired early and moved to the North Carolina mountains where she lives with her husband and a little black cat named Molly. CR loves the outdoors, reads too much, and writes too little. A realist with two feet planted in the 21st century, she nevertheless enjoys escaping into the past with historical fiction. *Jane Digby's Diary, A Rebel Heart* is her second novel.